Born
to
Dance

Born to Dance

Jean Ure

HarperCollins *Children's Books*

First published in Great Britain by HarperCollins *Children's Books* 2017
HarperCollins *Children's Books* is a division of HarperCollins*Publishers* Ltd,
1 London Bridge Street, London SE1 9GF

The HarperCollins *Children's Books* website address is:
www.harpercollins.co.uk

HarperCollins*Publishers*
1st Floor, Watermarque Building, Ringsend Road
Dublin 4, Ireland

ISBN 978-0-00-816452-2

Typeset by Palimpsest Book Production Ltd, Falkirk, Stirlingshire

Printed and bound by
CPI Group (UK) Ltd, Croydon, CR0 4YY

Chapter One

I knew the minute I saw her that Caitlyn was a dancer. Even though she was just sitting there quite quietly in the front hall, along with the other new girls, I could tell. There was just something about her. It was the way she sat — straight-backed, but perfectly relaxed, knees neatly together, hands lightly clasped in her lap. Very calm and poised.

On one side of her there was a tall, athletic-looking girl with her legs sprawled out and her hands dangling down like she'd forgotten they were there. *Not* very elegant! On the other side was a tiny, bright-eyed thing with a mop of dark curls, who was swinging her feet to and fro and nibbling at a thumbnail. Probably suffering from new-school nerves. Caitlyn said a lot later that she had been, too, though you would never have guessed it.

"What do you reckon?" hissed Livi.

We were standing at the top of the stairs, Livi and me and Jordan, peering down into the hall. We weren't supposed to be at the top of the stairs, we were supposed to be making our way to our classroom, but it was the beginning of the autumn term when new girls would be starting, especially in Year Seven. Who could resist the temptation to have a bit of a sneak peek?

"That one looks like she could be OK," said Jordan, nodding in the direction of the tall girl.

"Or the little one," said Liv.

Jordan agreed that she might be fun. Neither of them bothered with Caitlyn; it was almost like she didn't exist. Where I saw a fellow dancer, they just saw someone small and pale and insignificant. In other words, *boring*.

The office door opened and Mrs Betts appeared. Mrs Betts is our school secretary and a lot fiercer than any of the teachers. She glanced at the three of us at the top of the stairs and frowned slightly, like, *Isn't it time you were in class?* We drew back, guiltily.

"You coming?" said Jordan.

I said, "Yes, OK! I'm coming."

I stayed just long enough to watch as Caitlyn and the others made their way across the hall. I was right: Caitlyn had a dancer's walk! Even down to what Jordan and Livi insist on calling splay-feet, just to tease me. Actually it's flat-footed people who have splay-feet: dancers have *turn-out*. There's a huge difference. With splay-feet you *flump*. Caitlyn didn't flump. She was elegant!

Of course at that point I didn't know her name, but I was already wondering where she went for lessons. I knew all of the local dance schools. I also knew lots of the people who went to them. The world of dance is quite a small one. I thought perhaps, looking at her, that she might go to Miss Hennessy, who was the only other teacher Mum considered reputable. The only other teacher besides Mum herself, that is! She was always very scathing about the rest of them, especially

The Dance Bug, with its ridiculous purple uniform and glossy brochures. She said it turned out nothing but robots.

"All technique and no soul."

As for Babette Wynstan and her Babette's Babes — always strutting their stuff in the local pantomime — well! I couldn't repeat the things Mum said about them. It's true that Mum is a bit of a snob where ballet is concerned, but wherever Caitlyn went for classes it looked to me like she had been well taught.

Her name, as I discovered in registration, was Caitlyn Hughes. A good name, I thought, for a dancer. Mum once had a pupil called Martha Roope. How could you get anywhere with a name like that? And I once read that Margot Fonteyn started off as Peggy Hookham. I couldn't believe it! *Peggy Hookham.*

The part of the Swan Queen was danced to perfection by Peggy Hookham...

I don't think so! I was so amazed when I discovered this that I excitedly reported it to Livi and Jordan.

"Did you know that Margot Fonteyn started off as Peggy Hookham?"

I confidently expected them to squeal and go, "Peggy Hookham?"

But they just stared at me in total blankness and said, "Who's Margot Fonteyn?" I'm not even sure they didn't say *Margaret* Fonteyn. *Un-be-liev-able!*

I snapped, "She was only one of the all-time greats!" How could anyone not have heard of Margot Fonteyn? People are amazingly ignorant when it comes to ballet. I'd been friends with Livi and Jordan ever since we'd started at Coombe House. We always shared secrets and hung out together and stuck up for one another, but they still couldn't tell a *jeté* from an arabesque, and didn't have had the least idea what a *pas de bourrée* was. As for never having heard of Margot Fonteyn... words fail me!

I watched that morning as Caitlyn filed into assembly with the rest of us. I thought that she would know who Margot Fonteyn was! I liked the idea of having a fellow dancer to chat with. The only other girl in our class who did ballet had left, and she hadn't been what Mum would call a proper dancer, anyway. Just one of Babette's Babes. Mention Babette to Mum and she goes, "Well, if you want to train *chorus* girls…" Meaning not proper corps de ballet, just Babette's Babes, all simpering and kicking their legs in the air.

At first break I went bounding up to Caitlyn, dragging Livi and Jordan with me. I said, "'Scuse me! Where do you do ballet?"

Caitlyn said, "Ballet?" She sounded startled, like I'd caught her out in some kind of crime. Maybe I'd been too eager. Mum is always accusing me of blundering around like a bull in a china shop.

I said, "Yes, sorry! I'm Maddy, by the way. I didn't mean to be nosy – I just wondered which school you went to."

Caitlyn hesitated, as if she didn't quite know what to say.

"Dance school," I added.

"Actually she *is* being nosy," said Jordan, "but she

can't help it. It's not her fault, poor thing. Her whole family is, like, *obsessed*."

"Her mum," said Livi, giving me a little poke, as if perhaps she might be referring to someone else's mum, "has her own ballet school. She used to be a ballerina! So did her dad – well!" She giggled. "Not a *ballerina*, obviously!"

"Ballet *dancer*," said Jordan.

"Ballet *dancer*," agreed Liv. "And now he makes up ballets for other people. He goes all over the world. Doesn't he?" She turned to me. I nodded, reluctantly. Why were we talking about my dad? How did he come into it? It was Caitlyn I wanted to know about! "He's even been to Moscow," said Liv, proudly.

"Yes, and her brother," said Jordan, "is a *preema* dancer!"

"*Premier danseur*," I said. And anyway he wasn't. He was too young to be a *premier danseur*. He'd only just been promoted to soloist.

"He's a star," said Liv. "And her sister—"

"Is having a baby," I said.

"Yes, but before that *she* was a star! All Maddy's family are stars. That's why—"

"Oh, do shut up about my family," I begged. "Nobody's in the least bit interested."

Certainly not Caitlyn. She couldn't have made it more obvious. If she'd been interested, she'd have wanted to know what my surname was, and I'd have said O'Brien and then she'd have put two and two together and realised that my dad must be Declan, and my brother was Sean. She might even have remembered that my sister was Jenny and that Mum had been Yvette Anderson. And she would *certainly* have heard of the Anderson Academy of Dance! Except—

She'd been there, hadn't she, when we had registration? She'd have heard my name read out – Madeleine O'Brien. So, if she was a dancer, she'd surely have put two and two together right away? Just for a moment I thought perhaps I'd got it wrong. But I hadn't! I was sure I hadn't. Caitlyn was a dancer if ever I saw one. She had to be! When you have a mum who runs a ballet school and a dad who's a choreographer, when your *entire family* is into ballet, you can recognise a fellow dancer when you see one.

By now the silence was becoming too embarrassing even for me. In what I hoped were dignified tones I said, "I'm so sorry. I didn't mean to pry, it's just that I know all the local teachers and I couldn't help wondering..." My voice trailed off. Lamely I said, "I just wondered where you took lessons."

"Ballet lessons," said Jordan, encouragingly.

"I don't do *ballet*," said Caitlyn. She said it quite rudely. Almost like, *Who in their right mind would want to do anything so girly?*

Some people do think that ballet is girly. They have no idea of all the training you have to go through and all the hard work you have to put in. They think it's nothing but pointing your toes and wearing fluffy skirts. Was that what Caitlyn thought?

I almost never blush but I could feel my cheeks fire

up. I felt like I'd been slapped in the face. I'd only meant to be friendly!

"Sorry," I muttered. Not, to be honest, that I saw any reason to apologise. I was just showing an interest! Showing an interest isn't the same as being nosy. "I really thought you looked like a dancer."

"Well, I'm not," said Caitlyn.

Jordan slipped her arm through mine. "Let's go," she said.

Meekly I allowed myself to be led away.

"Really!" said Livi. "What a thoroughly unpleasant person."

"Won't bother with *her* again," agreed Jordan. "Dunno what made you go and talk to her in the first place."

Pleadingly I said, "I really thought she was a dancer."

I still thought she was a dancer. Why wouldn't she admit it?

"Doesn't look much like a dancer to me," said Livi.

"That one could be." Jordan nodded across the yard to where the tiny girl with the bright eyes was standing with the big, athletic-looking one. Ava, her name was. The other was Astrid.

I shook my head. "She's way too small."

"Too *small*?" Jordan's voice rose to a squeak. "How can she be too small?"

"That Caitlyn's hardly a giant," said Livi. She sniffed. "Skinny thing!"

Caitlyn was what I would've called exactly right. Right height, right shape. About the same as me, in fact. Mum has always monitored all of us most carefully, terrified that we'd end up too short or too tall. You don't want extremes in a ballet company, except maybe for soloists. But nobody starts off as a soloist. Pretty well everyone has to begin in the corps, and you can't very well have six-foot dancers and four-foot dancers all muddled up together – it would ruin the line.

The bell had rung for the end of break and I watched, critically, as Ava set off across the yard. She bounced as she walked. Bibbity-bob, bibbity-bob, with her head nodding up and down. Quite cute! But not a dancer's walk. Caitlyn, on the other hand... I looked around in time to catch her going back into school. She was so graceful. She *had* to be a dancer! I didn't care what she said.

It was a puzzle, and I couldn't help feeling a bit disappointed. It would have been fun to have someone to talk ballet with. Even sometimes, maybe, to practise with. Livi and Jordan meant well, but they had no idea what it was actually like, training to be a dancer. Still I didn't intend to go back for a second helping. I am not a person who bears grudges — I honestly don't believe that I am — but once is enough. I'd tried to be friendly, and she'd made it quite plain that she didn't want to know.

I pointedly didn't take any notice of Caitlyn after that. At least I tried not to, but I still found myself watching her at odd moments, like in morning assembly or out in the yard at break. It didn't help that her desk was directly in front of mine in class, which meant I could hardly avoid studying the back of her head. A dancer's head! There are all different types of heads. Big ones, like turnips; small ones, like tennis balls. Round ones, oval ones, lumpy ones, bumpy ones. Caitlyn's was small and shapely, perfectly balanced on a long, slender neck. Just right for ballet!

It was really frustrating. I still couldn't believe I'd got it so wrong. I might almost have been tempted to break my vow and try talking to her again, but Livi and Jordan made sure I didn't get the chance.

"Just ignore her," said Liv. "People who are that rude aren't worth bothering with."

"I mean, so *insulting*," said Jordan.

"Ungracious," said Liv. She is rather into these literary sort of words. It's cos of her dad being this big, important professor of English. "You'd have thought she'd feel *proud* being at school with someone from a famous family."

I mumbled a protest. "My family aren't famous."

"We think they are," said Jordan.

I said, "Sean might be, one day." Even I might be, one day!

"Are you telling me," said Liv, "that people don't know who your mum and dad are?"

"Well... *some* people," I said. "Ballet people."

"We're not ballet people," said Jordan.

"No, but you're my friends," I said.

And being my friends they did sometimes have this tendency to boast a little. To new girls, for instance, such as Caitlyn. But it wasn't like *I* was boasting! There really wasn't any reason for Caitlyn to have been so unpleasant.

For all that, I still couldn't stop studying the back of her head. I still refused to believe she wasn't a dancer.

I tried talking to Mum about it after class that evening. I said, "There's this new girl started at school. She's called Caitlyn. She swears she doesn't do ballet but I don't believe her! I'm sure she does."

Mum said, "Really?" Not, unfortunately, in a very interested sort of way. More like, *Why is she telling me this now?* It probably wasn't the best moment to try talking to her about Caitlyn, when she'd been teaching all day and half the evening and just wanted to get home. But it's never a best moment with Mum. She's very... absorbed in her work, is what Liv would say.

I waited while Mum locked up and we walked out to the car. I said, "Why would anyone lie about it?"

"About what?" said Mum.

"Learning ballet!"

"Oh, goodness knows. People have their reasons. Incidentally, I meant to say earlier, you really must put in some work on your *ports de bras*. You're getting very sloppy!"

I pulled a face. I know that arms are not my strongest point.

"Did you hear me?" said Mum.

I said, "Yes. I heard you."

"Well, don't just talk about it," said Mum. "See to it!"

"I will," I said. "I will!"

I always give up, in the end. You simply can't have a conversation with Mum that isn't directly to do with ballet. Dad isn't very much better. No use expecting either of them to shed any light on the mystery. But I do so hate to be wrong!

On Thursday the following week, when we'd been back at school for ten days (and I was still hypnotically staring at the back of Caitlyn's head), it poured with rain and we had to do PE in the gym. Coombe House is a very small school; we don't have proper sports facilities. Just a single court where we can play netball or tennis, plus a patch of grass for rounders. No hockey. Certainly no football. So, when it rains, we all have to go up to the gym, where there isn't very much except a few wall bars and a bit of coconut matting.

Miss Lucas, our PE teacher, is quite ancient and what she likes best is to get us all swaying about in time to music, or doing strange, bendy exercises – "Stretch, girls! As high as you can!" Sometimes we do a bit of dancing: old-fashioned stuff like polkas and waltzes. Stuff that anyone can do. But still Miss Lucas always goes, "Watch, girls! All look at Maddy!" Really embarrassing. There was this one time she said we were going to do Greek dancing and we got all fired up with enthusiasm, cos Greek dancing is fun, at least all the Greek dancing I've ever seen. I was all ready to fling myself into it, and this time I wouldn't have minded if Miss Lucas wanted people to watch me. I'm really good at character dancing! But then all it turned out to be was just wandering about, striking weird poses. No real dancing at all.

I got a bit bold, cos it was, like, really frustrating, and shouted, "It's not like *Zorba the Greek*!" *Zorba the Greek* is this film that Dad has in his collection and which I know practically off by heart. They do *real* dancing in that. But when I told Mum, expecting her to be sympathetic, she said it was not only extremely rude of me but also unkind.

"Poor old soul," she said. "She does her best."

"But Mum," I wailed, "it was just *stupid!*"

"So learn to put up with it," said Mum. "Behave yourself!"

I do try, but when you're told to "hop like a kangaroo" or "bounce like a ball" it's very difficult to take it seriously, especially when you're used to the discipline of barre work, with Mum prowling about the studio, watching your every move with her hawk-like eye.

That Thursday, after the usual stretching and skipping, Miss Lucas said she wanted us to walk across the floor as though on a tightrope above Cheddar Gorge.

"High, high up!" She wafted her hands above her head to demonstrate. I giggled, and immediately stifled it. I like Miss Lucas; I would never want to hurt her feelings. But it really did make me feel like I was back to being four years old and just starting my first dancing class. It's all very well being kangaroos and bouncing balls when you're four years old; not when you're eleven and have been studying ballet for almost as long as you can remember. But Mum had said to behave myself so I obediently went off to the far end of the gym to make like I was crossing Cheddar Gorge.

I glanced at Caitlyn out of the corner of my eye to see how she was taking it. She seemed quite happy, lost in a world of her own. High up among imaginary clouds, no doubt. I shrugged. What would Dad do, I wondered, if he was making a ballet about tightrope walkers? He would be bound to have *one* person who was a bit uncertain. Like in *Les Patineurs*, which is a skating ballet, where one of the skaters goes *flump!* on to her bottom. I couldn't very well go *flump* and fall into Cheddar Gorge, but I could be a bit wobbly. More than a bit wobbly! I could miss my footing. I could slip, I could slide, I could almost fall off. *Eee... ow... aaaargh!*

I knew it wasn't what Miss Lucas wanted. She wanted us all to be beautifully poised and balanced, like the time she'd got us walking around the gym with books on our head. But you have to have *some* fun!

When we'd all successfully walked our tightropes across the yawning gulf beneath us, Miss Lucas said,

"Right! Let's all watch Maddy." She nodded at me. "Off you go!"

I think by now people were used to me being singled out. They were kind of resigned to it. There wasn't anyone else in the class who was a dancer, or even wanted to be a dancer, so perhaps they didn't really care.

I wobbled back along my imaginary tightrope. I slipped and tripped and threw up my arms in horror. People laughed. I did it again, and they laughed again, so I pulled this agonised face and began to step *reeeeally sloooowly*, trying not to look down, cos if you looked down... *Eee... ow... aaaargh!* That was nearly it. *Phew!*

Everybody by now was in fits of giggles. Miss Lucas gave a little smile. She said, "Well, I think you'll all agree that was very clever. Thank you, Maddy! Now... Caitlyn." She beckoned. "Not quite so clever, maybe, but... let's see what people think. Come! Don't be nervous."

Caitlyn had turned bright pink. I wondered what Miss Lucas had meant when she'd said, "Not quite so clever *but...*" Like maybe clever wasn't such a good thing?

"Off you go," said Miss Lucas.

Caitlyn set off diagonally across the gym. We all watched, like in some kind of trance. You could almost feel the wire stretched taut beneath her feet, just as you could almost sense the gaping void beneath her. If she'd been in a film, instead of in the gym, it would have been enough to make you hold your breath. I think some people actually did hold their breath, cos the minute she reached the end and stepped off there was a loud burst of applause. Even Miss Lucas joined in. After a few seconds (to get over my surprise) I did, too.

"So, there you are," said Miss Lucas. "Two very different interpretations. Maddy used technique, Caitlyn her imagination. We laughed at one and held our breath with the other."

Liv and Jordan grumbled afterwards.

"What on earth was she on about? You used your imagination just as much as she did!"

But I hadn't; Miss Lucas was right. I *had* relied on technique. If I'd used imagination, people wouldn't have laughed: they would have been holding their breath, just as they had for Caitlyn.

Why did I feel that I'd let myself down?

Chapter Two

Next morning I was told that Miss Lucas wanted to see me in the gym at lunchtime.

"Wonder what that's about?" said Livi.

I pulled a face. She was probably going to talk to me about yesterday, about what Mum would have called my "antics" on the high wire. Mum doesn't approve of antics; she says they are just a way of showing off. Mum's pupils are not expected to show off. We leave all that sort of thing to Babette's Babes, sashaying about the stage in their sparkly tiaras and pretty little pink tutus.

Miss Lucas is softer than Mum, and a whole lot kinder. She wouldn't fix me with a contemptuous stare and coldly ask me what on earth I thought I was doing. Mum would! Miss Lucas would just be very sad and reproachful, which in some ways was even worse as it would make me feel ashamed of myself, especially if she gazed at me with her sorrowful eyes. Like, *How could you do that to me, Maddy?* Like she knew I secretly considered myself too grand to go skipping and hopping and tiptoeing about on imaginary tightropes.

I'd already made up my mind that I would apologise. I would admit that Mum is always accusing me of playing for laughs. I would be humble and meekly accept that it is one of my worst faults. I am never meek with Mum! She can sometimes make me quite defiant. But Miss Lucas is so gentle you almost feel the need to protect her.

"Ah, Maddy," she said, as I presented myself in the gym. "Thank you for coming! I'm so sorry to cut into your lunch hour."

I said, "That's all right." I was a bit taken aback, to

tell the truth. I'd thought I was the one who was supposed to apologise!

"I wanted to talk to you," said Miss Lucas, "about the Christmas production."

"Oh?" I perked up. Maybe she was going to offer me one of the lead parts. Fingers crossed! After all, I was in senior school now, so she surely couldn't expect me to do what I'd done last year, and the year before, when she'd wanted me to perform little soppy dances to steps that she'd made up. Not when I was in Year Seven!

"Let's sit down," said Miss Lucas.

We both sank down on to the coconut matting and sat with our legs crossed. I had to fight another of my horrible urges to giggle. Miss Lucas is older than my gran! I couldn't imagine my gran sitting cross-legged on coconut matting. But I suppose Miss Lucas is still quite supple for an older person.

"I thought that this year," she said, her eyes gleaming with excitement, "we'd do a real play... a Christmas play. One that I've written myself."

I made a little noise like "Mm!" to show that I was impressed. Miss Lucas beamed.

"Let me tell you what it's about."

It was about a Christmas tree fairy who had become old and tattered. Once upon a time she had been young and beautiful. Every year she had been brought down from her box in the attic with all the rest of the Christmas decorations and placed at the top of the tree. Now the family who owned her didn't want her any more.

"Four little rich girls," said Miss Lucas. "All horribly spoilt! '*Ugh, Mum, look at it!*' they go." Miss Lucas put on a little girly voice. Little *rich* girly voice. All shrill and shrieky. "'*You'll have to get us a new one, Mum! We can't invite all our friends to our Christmas party with that disgusting old thing at the top of the tree!*' And so," continued Miss Lucas, "they take the poor fairy and they throw her out with the rubbish." Miss Lucas made a throwing motion. "'*Tatty old thing!*'"

She leaned forward, very earnestly. "They're not very

nice girls, you see, but they don't really know any better, poor things! They've been brought up to believe that the minute something becomes a bit worn or a bit dirty it's no good any more."

I nodded, solemnly. I wasn't going to tell her that last Christmas I'd begged Mum and Dad for new decorations cos ours were starting to look all old and shabby!

"That poor fairy," said Miss Lucas. "She's so unhappy! Cast out of the only home she's ever known... rejected by the family she loves. Can you imagine it, Maddy? Can you imagine how she must feel?"

Miss Lucas fixed me with a tragic gaze. Her eyes were swimming. I made another encouraging "Mm!" sound. *Maybe*, I thought, *I could play one of the spoilt little rich girls.* I'd enjoy that! "So, there she is," said Miss Lucas, "tossed out with the rubbish. All alone in the cold and the dark. But wait!" She flung up a hand. "What's this sniffing around the bin? It's a fox!" Miss Lucas clasped her hands to her bosom. I clasped mine as well, to show that I was living it with her. "He drags the poor fairy out and starts playing with her... tossing her about—"

We both made tossing motions.

"Until, in the end—" Miss Lucas sank back, "—he tires of the game. He drops her in the gutter – *plosh!* – and goes running off. The poor little soul is left there, face down—" Miss Lucas drooped. "She's cold; she's wet; her once beautiful skirt is torn and muddy. Her poor heart is broken."

I said, "That is really sad." I wondered if it was a part that I would want to play. Being broken-hearted is not really my thing. I mean, I *could* be, obviously. But it's not what I'm best at.

"Anyway," said Miss Lucas, "time passes and we cut to a different family... a mum and her three children. Two little girls, one little boy. Well! The boy isn't that little. About your age, I'd say."

I sat up, bright and expectant. Maybe I could play the boy? I'd be good at playing a boy!

"This is an underprivileged family," said Miss Lucas. "Dad's no longer around; Mum is on her own. They're having to live in a B & B."

Excuse me? I obviously looked puzzled.

"*Bed and breakfast.*" Miss Lucas whispered it, as if it was too dreadful to say out loud. "Sometimes they even have to visit a *food bank*. What kind of Christmas can they look forward to?"

"Not a very nice one," I said.

"Not a very nice one at all! No tree, no fairy... hardly anything in the way of presents. One little girl isn't very well, and she does *so* want a tree. And a fairy to go on top! But Mum can't afford it."

Sadly Miss Lucas shook her head. I waited, expectantly. At least she couldn't ask me to play the sick little girl; she'd need someone younger for that.

"So next," said Miss Lucas, "we have a scene where the little boy is walking along the road, scuffing his feet, miserable because he can't do anything to help his little sister."

I nodded. I could scuff my feet! And kick things. Little boys were always kicking things.

"I think probably," said Miss Lucas, "that both this scene and the one with the fox—"

I had a moment of horror. *Please, please,* I thought, *don't ask me to play the part of a fox!*

"I can see you looking worried," said Miss Lucas. "You're asking yourself, how do we portray a fox? I'm sure it can be done. There's a girl in Year Six—"

Oh, I thought. *Lucky her!*

"Anyway, as I was saying, I think those two scenes should both take place in front of the curtain. What do you think?"

Like I was some kind of expert! I said, "Yes, that's an excellent idea. Cos they'd be street scenes."

"Exactly." Miss Lucas looked pleased. "I thought we could get the art department to paint a suitable backcloth... houses, shops. That kind of thing."

"That would be really good," I said.

"It would, wouldn't it? We obviously think alike! So,

there's the little boy, wandering along, when suddenly he catches sight of something in the gutter... what can it be?"

"The fairy?" I said.

"The fairy! Poor, wet, bedraggled fairy. To cut a long story short," said Miss Lucas, "he rescues her, takes her back with him. Mum helps clean her up, even manages to make her a new skirt and mend her wand, while the little boy uses silver foil to turn an old abandoned umbrella into... guess what? A Christmas tree! Such a wonderful surprise for his little sisters when they wake up on Christmas morning! *'Is she really ours?'*" whispered Miss Lucas. "'*Can we keep her?*' Mum assures them that they can. So, all ends well for everybody! The little girls have their Christmas tree fairy, and the Christmas tree fairy has a new family to love her. What do you think?"

She looked at me, eagerly. I struggled to find something to say. To me it seemed a bit... mushy. Like when I'm forced to eat something I hate, such as Brussels sprouts, just to take one particularly loathsome example, and I smash them all up with the potatoes and the gravy so that Mum accuses me of making a mush. Miss Lucas's story was a mush! All soft and squishy and kind of *yuck*. But she was so pleased with it! She was so happy!

"Of course," she said hastily, "there will be other scenes. I thought maybe in the penultimate scene – that is, the next to last, before we have the little boy and his family waking up on Christmas morning – I thought it might be nice to show the rich little girls having a party. They could invite all their friends and show off their new expensive fairy, but oh, dear!" Miss Lucas rolled her eyes. "These rich little girls will squabble so! They all want to be the one to put the fairy on the tree. They end up quarrelling so badly that their mother has to come in and put a stop to it."

In that case, I thought, *I'd like to play one of the little rich girls*. The oldest one. I already saw her as being very bossy and snatching at the fairy and jumping on a chair so she could reach the top of the tree. But then maybe one of the others would grab at her and pull her down and they'd end up fighting and pulling hair and scratching. Yes! I could turn her into a really spoilt brat.

"Well?" Miss Lucas was waiting anxiously for me to say something.

"It sounds really good," I said. "Which part did you want me to play? Shall I be the oldest sister?"

"Oh, Maddy, no!" cried Miss Lucas. "You're our little dancer! What I want from you, I want to have a dance interlude between the acts. It would be after the poor fairy's been thrown out. She'd be so sad. So very sad! She'd remember the old days, when she was young and the girls loved her. She might even do a few steps, trying to recapture the magic of her youth..."

Miss Lucas made a frail gesture with one arm. Her head drooped, her shoulders sagged. She looked a bit like Anna Pavlova in *The Dying Swan*. I fought back another surge of giggles. I'd promised Mum I'd behave myself! And it wasn't fair to laugh just cos I thought her idea was mushy. My only fear was how much *more* mushy would her dance interlude turn out to be?

"Naturally—" she suddenly snapped back into brisk, teacherly mode "—it would be entirely up to you. I wouldn't want to interfere. You would have complete freedom. I'm sure you're a far more capable choreographer than I am!"

I blinked. "You want me to make up my own steps?"

"Oh, Maddy, *could* you?" Miss Lucas clasped both hands back to her bosom. (I say bosom as it is only polite, though in fact she is so skinny she is like a tube.) "That would be really wonderful! You're so much more advanced than you were last year. I couldn't possibly do justice to your talents! But of course," she added, "you must ask your mother. If she thinks it's too much, you must say so. I know how busy you are, with your lessons."

I wasn't as busy as all that. I *could* find the time. But I did so wish that just for once I could play a speaking part! Maybe I could get Mum to say she'd rather I didn't take on any more dance assignments but wouldn't mind if I was one of the spoilt sisters.

"So, what do you think?" said Miss Lucas.

I promised that I would ask Mum. "I'll see what she says."

This time I waited for a good moment. Mum had taken her last class of the day and was back home, with a glass of wine and her feet up. Sean wasn't there cos he was at the theatre, and Dad was on his way to New York to mount a production of *ZigZag*, one of his most popular works, for the New York City Ballet. I had Mum all to myself. I just wanted her to agree that it wouldn't be sensible for me to take on any more work. *Dancing* work.

"Cos, you know, having to do all the choreography... I couldn't properly give it my full attention."

"Why not?" said Mum. I said, "Well, I mean..." I waved a hand. "What with classes and everything."

"What's everything?" said Mum.

"*Practising. Ports de bras*, like you said! And schoolwork. I have to do *some* schoolwork."

Mum said, "Maddy, you have the very minimum amount of schoolwork. It's one of the reasons we sent you there, so you'd have plenty of time for your dancing."

"But classes!" I wailed.

"Two a week plus Saturday mornings? That's nothing! When I was your age," said Mum, "I was leaving home for a seven o'clock class every morning."

"Not when you were eleven," I said.

"I would have done," said Mum, "if it had been asked of me."

"Well, anyway." I flopped down at the far end of the sofa. Mum hastily transferred her glass from one hand to the other.

"Just watch what you're doing, Maddy! You're supposed to be a dancer... *Gracious. Poised.* Not hurling yourself about like a baby elephant."

"Sorry." I could already sense that this was not going to go well. "Thing is—" I picked at a bit of sofa which seemed to be coming loose. "Thing is, it's a really soppy storyline! I just don't know what I'm supposed to do with it. It's about this—"

"Stop!" Mum held up a hand. She never has much patience with what she calls "moaning and carrying on". "Whatever it's about I'm sure you'll find a way to deal with it. It'll be good experience for you."

"It might be," I said, "if I wanted to be a choreographer. But I don't!"

"Do you think your dad knew that that's what he wanted at your age?"

I frowned. What did Dad have to do with it?

"You just never know," said Mum. "And think how happy it will make Miss Lucas!"

I plucked some more at the sofa. "It won't make her happy if I'm just, like, totally uninspired."

"I should certainly hope you *won't* be totally uninspired!"

"But I don't know how long she wants it to be! I don't even have any music! I—"

"So find some," snapped Mum "Heaven knows your

dad has a large enough collection. And stop pulling the furniture to pieces!"

I said, "Sorry! But honestly I can't see there's any *point* in having a dance interlude."

"Why not?" said Mum. "If that's what Miss Lucas wants... It's her show. And you *are* a dancer, so why not make use of you?"

"But Mum, she wants me to be a fairy!" I said.

"So? What's wrong with that? I'll have you know," said Mum, "that the Lilac Fairy was one of my very first solo roles!"

I said, "That's different. That's in *Sleeping Beauty*. That's a classic! This is just soppy."

"It doesn't have to be," said Mum. "You're the one doing the choreography; it's up to you. You can't have it both ways! You complain when you're asked to do it yourself and you complain when Miss Lucas does it for you. All that fuss last year at having to do that pathetic little dance she'd made up!"

I said, "Yes, cos it was tacky. *You* said so."

"Well, all right, it was. But Miss Lucas is not a professional dancer: you are. Or at least you're aiming to be. I would expect you to do a bit better than Miss Lucas. This is an opportunity, Maddy! Make the most of it. You could start by finding some suitable music. That's always your dad's way in. Find the music and let it inspire you."

I heaved a sigh. I had so wanted, this one time, to have a proper speaking part! Just to show what I could do. Everybody knew I could dance. I wanted to show them I could act as well!

"Music!" said Mum.

I said, "Yes. All right."

I supposed it would have to be something slow and mournful. I would obviously have to waft about the stage looking pathetic, with lyrical arm movements and maybe the occasional arabesque. Nothing in the least bit exciting. Certainly no *fouettés* or pirouettes. Just boring *adage*. Slow, slow, *slow*. Exactly what I am least good at!

I went through Dad's music collection and found some slow, sad music and waited for it to inspire me. But it didn't! There are some dancers who are just naturally gifted at *adage*. They have beautiful lines and what Mum calls "poise and serenity". Then there are others – like me – who shine at *allegro*. We leap, we spin, we turn, we dazzle. But how could a broken-down fairy do any of that?

And then, as I sat on the floor, brooding over the slow, sad music and waiting for inspiration, I remembered something Miss Lucas had said. *She'd remember the old days, when she was young... She might even do a few steps, trying to recapture the magic of her youth.*

Yesss! I sprang up, suddenly excited. That would be my way in! The fairy leaping and spinning, just as she had when she was young. *Now* I was inspired! All I had to do was find some music. Something fast and zingy. Of course it would only be a dream. An old, tired fairy wouldn't really have the energy to perform *fouettées* and *entrechats* and *grands jetés* all over the place. But that was all right: she would be *remembering*. It would be a dream sequence. Dad had a dream sequence in one of his ballets; there wasn't anything wrong with it. It wouldn't be showing off. It wouldn't be *cheating*. It would show the audience what the fairy had once been capable of. And, of course, to show them what I was capable of. Why not? I was the choreographer!

Chapter Three

Now that I'd decided what to do I found myself fizzing with enthusiasm. I wondered if this was how Dad felt when he began working on a new ballet. It was exciting! Especially once I'd found the right music, all zippy and fast-moving, with sudden trumpet blasts and spiky rhythms. Mum was right: music was the starting point! My head was a whirl of steps and sequences; I just needed space to try them out.

I did consider asking Mum if I could borrow one of her studios, but then I thought maybe that wasn't such a good idea. Mum would always be looking in on me to see how I was getting on and to offer advice. I didn't want that! This was going to be *my* choreography, done entirely by *me*. So then I had the much better idea of asking Miss Lucas if I could use the gym.

She was delighted. I knew she would be!

"Maddy," she said, "I'm so happy that you're doing this! By all means use the gym. Do you want it before school or after?"

I said that it would have to be before cos of after-school lessons with Mum.

"But if I could come in really early in the morning? Like half past seven maybe?"

"No problem," said Miss Lucas. "There's always someone around. I'll arrange it with Mrs Betts. Just remember to sign in at the Office so we know you're here."

Mum was quite impressed when I told her I'd need to be leaving an hour earlier every morning. She even said she'd give me a lift.

"I don't mind getting to the studio a bit earlier. It'll give me a chance to catch up with myself."

* * *

School was very strange and deserted so early in the morning, though Mrs Betts was there, and some of the teachers. I could also see a group of Year Twelves practising on the netball court and hear the tinkling of someone having a piano lesson in one of the music rooms. I was already wearing my leotard and tights under my coat, so I went straight up to the gym with my shoes and a couple of CDs I'd brought with me. One of them was my lovely zingy music, the other was a CD Mum had put together for workouts. My plan was to work out for fifteen minutes then spend the rest of the time getting the jumble of steps out of my brain and into my feet. I was itching to try them out!

And then, as I reached the gym, I stopped. What was going on in there? I could hear what sounded like someone moving about. Not loud enough to be an actual noise: more like the sliding of feet on the gym floor, followed by a soft *thunk*.

I opened the door, very gently, and peered through. What I saw was such a shock that I almost let the door go thudding shut again. A small figure, dressed like me in leotard and tights, was dancing in the centre of the gym. It was Caitlyn!

She seemed to be attempting pirouettes, though not very successfully. Not very successfully *at all*. I could see at once what the problem was: she was so busy concentrating on the position of her arms and legs that she was forgetting to find a spot to fix her eyes on. You can't do turns without spotting! Surely whoever her teacher was must have told her?

"'Scuse me!"

I'd gone racing into the gym before I could stop myself. I could see, afterwards, that it would have been more diplomatic to stay outside and clear my throat or rattle the door handle, to give her some warning. But I was just so surprised!

Caitlyn spun around, startled, as I burst in.

"Are you trying to practise pirouettes?" I said.

"No!" Her face immediately turned crimson. "It was just... just something I..."

What? Something she what? She didn't stay long enough to say. Just gave a little gasp and scuttled for the door.

"I'm sorry! I know I shouldn't be here!"

"You can be here!" I cried. But too late: she was already on her way out.

In her rush I saw that she'd left her outdoor shoes behind. I snatched them up and ran after her.

"Caitlyn!" I called out, over the banisters. She paused, and glanced up. "Here!" I tossed the shoes down to her. "You don't have to go," I said.

For a moment she hesitated, but then violently shook her head and scurried on her way.

Slowly I went back into the gym. I put on Mum's CD and dutifully did my fifteen minutes of workout, but my brain was now buzzing with so many unanswered questions that I found it almost impossible to concentrate. *Why* was Caitlyn practising pirouettes in the gym? *Why* hadn't she been taught how to spot when doing turns? Why, after all, did she persist in saying she didn't do ballet when she quite obviously did?

All the rest of the day she kept away from me. At breaktime she stuck closely with the other two new girls: the tall one, Astrid, and the tiny one, Ava. I didn't want to barge in and start questioning her in front of other people. I'd already embarrassed her once, bulldozing my way into the gym. But I was just dying to get to the bottom of the mystery!

It wasn't till going-home time that I managed to get her on her own. I could see Mum waiting in the car outside the school gates, but I could also see Caitlyn just ahead of me. I raced after her.

"Hey, Caitlyn!"

She half turned. For a minute I thought she was going to take off, but reluctantly she waited for me.

"I don't mean to be nosy," I said, "but do tell me who your teacher is!"

"I don't have one." She said it almost desperately, like, *Please, please, just go away and leave me alone!*

I don't enjoy upsetting people. In spite of what Mum says, I am *not* insensitive – and, in any case, Mum is a fine one to talk – but how could I give up? *Now?* After what I had seen in the gym?

"Are you really saying you don't have classes?" I stared at her, exasperated. Why was she still denying it? Could it be that she was embarrassed cos of everyone knowing that my mum was one of the best teachers around, while hers quite obviously wasn't much good? Wasn't *any* good, on the evidence of those pirouettes!

"Well, you don't have to tell me if you don't want to," I said, "but I wish you'd stop pretending you don't do ballet when anybody can see that you do!"

As I said that, I thought I saw her eyes light up, but still she didn't say anything.

"Thing is," I said, "whoever's taught you pirouettes hasn't done it at all well. Didn't they tell you about spotting?"

"I know about spotting!" The words burst out of her. "I just can't seem to do it."

"It's easy," I said. "Honestly! Once you've been shown... it just takes a bit of practice. *I* could teach you!"

She bit her lip.

"I bet I could get you doing pirouettes in no time," I said.

I could see that she was tempted.

"Do you want to check first with your teacher?" I was being generous. I didn't reckon Caitlyn's teacher, whoever she was, deserved to be consulted. "P'raps if you tell her who I am – not meaning to boast," I said hurriedly, "but I do know what I'm doing! I've been having lessons with Mum since I was four years old. If we met up in the gym really early, like *really* early, like seven o'clock, maybe, cos we'd have to warm up first, then afterwards I have to work on something for Miss Lucas, but before that we could do pirouettes. I just need some time for Miss Lucas's stuff. It's for her Christmas show. She wants me to make up a dance interlude for her! You could always stay and help me if you wanted? Like telling me what you think, and everything? That would be really helpful!"

I wasn't actually sure that it would be, though it's true I do enjoy having an audience. But mostly I wanted to encourage her. Make her feel welcome. She was obviously still uncertain.

"If you don't come," I said, "it's going to haunt me... you trying to do pirouettes and getting it all wrong. It *hurts* when you see someone who should be good at something being taught all wrong! Please, please, *please* let me show you how to do it properly!"

"All right." She suddenly sounded excited. "If you think it's really OK?"

"Why shouldn't it be?"

"Well... me being in the gym. Won't they mind?"

"Not if you're with me," I said. "I've got special permission. But don't worry, I'll ask Miss Lucas! I'll tell her you're helping. All we have to do is sign in every morning so they know we're here."

Out of the corner of my eye I could see that Liv had appeared and was coming over.

"OK," I said. "Deal?"

Caitlyn nodded. "Deal!"

"I'll see you tomorrow. Don't be late!"

I still hadn't solved the mystery but I was getting closer. I didn't particularly want Liv charging in and ruining everything. She and Jordan had developed a real hate thing about Caitlyn.

"What are you *doing*?" Liv demanded, as I turned in again through the gates. "Why were you talking to that horrible, rude girl and why are you going back into school?"

"I need to find Miss Lucas," I said. "And Caitlyn's not actually rude and horrible."

"Could've fooled me," said Liv. "What d'you want Miss Lucas for?"

Like it was any business of hers! But when you're friends with someone, when you've been friends for just about as long as you can remember, they seem to think they have a right to know every last detail of your life. I couldn't blame Liv; she didn't mean to pry. But I certainly wasn't going to explain about Caitlyn and the disastrous pirouettes! That would be like a betrayal.

I said, "I just have to check it's OK for me to come in early and use the gym. I need it to work on my choreography."

"Oh, the dance you're doing for the Christmas show! Can me and Jordan come and watch?"

"Not while I'm still working on it," I said. "I can't bear anyone to be around while I'm just trying things out."

Miss Lucas was more than happy for Caitlyn to join me for my early-morning sessions, though I could see she was a bit surprised.

"I didn't realise we had another little dancer, though come to think of it she certainly looks as if she could be one. I wonder if I ought to make up a little bit of dancing for her and one or two of the others? Perhaps at the end… just something simple. What do you think?"

I said, "I think it might be better if everybody came on and sang a carol maybe?"

I honestly did think it would be better than "a little bit of dancing" made up by Miss Lucas. She's a very sweet person, but the only steps she really knows are skipping and hopping and doing little twirls. Fortunately she liked the idea of a carol. It would round things off, she said. It would also give her the chance to include lots of people who wouldn't otherwise get to take part.

"I do like to open things up for as many as I can. Thank you for that suggestion, Maddy! It's all coming together, isn't it?"

By the time I got back to the gates, Mum was fretting and fuming. She's a very impatient kind of person.

"Maddy," she said, "where on earth have you been? I have a class starting in twenty minutes! *You* have a class starting in twenty minutes. What made you go rushing off like that?"

"Sorry," I said. "I forgot something. Mum, did you see that girl I was talking to?"

"What girl? I saw you with Livi."

"No, the one I was talking to before I went rushing off."

I was hoping Mum would say, *Oh, yes! The little dark-haired one who looks like a dancer.* Even Miss Lucas had recognised that Caitlyn looked like a dancer. But not Mum! Mum just said, vaguely, that she hadn't really noticed.

"Why, anyway?" she said. "Who is she?"

"She's the one I was telling you about... the one who says she doesn't do ballet but I now know that she obviously *does*."

"Oh, that one," said Mum, nosing the car out on to the main road. And then, before I could explain how I knew, "Will you just look at all that traffic! What in heaven's name is the hold-up?"

I sighed. It really is *very* difficult to get Mum's attention. She just sat there, fretting and fuming, and blaming me cos we were going to be late.

"It is *so* unprofessional! And what about those *ports*

de bras?" She turned, accusingly, to look at me. "Have you done anything about them?"

I said, "Yes, I've been practising."

"There'd better be some improvement. They were an absolute disgrace! There's no point having twinkly feet if your arms are like sausages."

Well, at least I had something. Twinkly feet! I could work on my arm movements, but there's not so much you can do about feet. They either twinkle or they don't. I wondered if Caitlyn's would twinkle. I had this feeling she would be more of an *adage* person, with a beautiful line and a perfect arabesque – unless her rotten teacher had let her down as badly over that as she had with pirouettes. I really hoped she hadn't! It would be such a waste of talent. Mum says there's no greater crime than waste of talent, and it's a well-known fact that bad habits are extremely difficult to put right. A poor teacher in your early years can be fatal. It can totally ruin someone.

* * *

I was a bit worried as I raced up the stairs to the gym next morning. Suppose Caitlyn had already been ruined? I might be raising her hopes for nothing, cos what would be the point of teaching her how to do pirouettes properly if everything else was wrong?

She was there, waiting for me, and I could see at once that she was anxious.

"It's all right," I said, sliding Mum's CD into the CD player. "We're just going to start with a bit of a warm-up... just a few *pliés* and *battements*, same as usual."

She nodded, nervously. I was quite nervous myself, even though I am not at all a nervous sort of person. Too confident for my own good is what Mum says.

I felt like Mum that morning. I found myself watching Caitlyn with hawk-like eyes, ready to pounce on the least little thing. *Relax those shoulders! Straighten that back! Watch those ankles!*

I was determined to be ruthless, just like Mum. I know it can be painful; I've seen Mum reduce people to floods of tears. Not me, cos I am made of sterner stuff. But for people who aren't too sure of themselves it can actually destroy them. Mum says this just goes to show they don't have what it takes. She is probably right, but I felt that I'd bullied Caitlyn into letting me see what she could do and I would really hate destroying her.

Thank goodness I didn't have to! Her shoulders were relaxed; her back was straight, her tummy flat, her bottom well tucked in. Best of all, her ankles didn't show any tendency to roll. She seemed to have perfect turn-out. Always a good sign!

I said, "Right." Very brisk, just like Mum. "Before I let you try any actual turns, I'm going to show you some exercises for focus. Eye focus. OK?"

She nodded, eagerly.

"This is the way I did it with Mum." Except that I'd done it when I was small, not when I was eleven years old! "Put your hands on your waist, and your feet together, then *bounce*. Now! Turn your head to the right and find a spot to look at... anything will do so long as you keep your eyes fixed on it while you turn. Like this!"

She watched, intently, as I demonstrated.

"The trick is to keep your eyes on the spot and whip your body round really fast so it catches up with your head... if you see what I mean."

She said, "Yes! I think so."

"OK! So, I want you to jump and do a quarter-turn to the right, keeping your eyes fixed like I showed you... There! How did it feel?"

"Um..." She sounded doubtful. "I don't think I'm doing it right!"

"Don't worry," I said. "It'll come. Honestly! It's the easiest thing in the world once you've got the hang of it. You'll find you can turn and turn and not even notice. Let's try again!"

And again, and again. I was determined not to give up.

"I'm being so stupid!" wailed Caitlyn.

"No, you're not," I said. "It's something you should have been taught ages ago, before you were allowed to even try doing any turns. *Nobody* can turn till they've learnt how to spot. I can't understand why you weren't taught! I know you don't want to tell me where you take classes," I said, "but wherever it is I don't think they should be teaching!"

Her cheeks by now were bright pink. I couldn't understand why she was so embarrassed. It was hardly her fault if she had a rotten teacher. Her mum should have checked out the school before sending her there. I wondered for a minute if it could possibly be the dreaded Babette Wynstan School of so-called Dance. They had a reputation for pushing people before they were properly prepared. But not even Babette would let her students attempt pirouettes without first teaching them how to focus. It was a real mystery! But for the moment I needed to concentrate all my energies on the task in hand.

"Again!" I said. "Keep those eyes fixed! *There.* That's it! You're doing it!"

Caitlyn's cheeks glowed, but with triumph this time.

I felt proud of us both! I could suddenly understand how Mum must feel when one of her students gets to grips with a step she's been having problems with.

"Did I do it right?" said Caitlyn.

"Absolutely!" I said. "You'll need more practice, but basically that's it. How did it feel? Did it feel good?"

Caitlyn nodded, blissfully.

"You can practise spotting while I practise my *ports de bras*," I said. "Mum got so angry with me! She said I'm a total disgrace. She says what's the point of having twinkly feet if your arms are like sausages?"

Caitlyn giggled. "You don't have arms like sausages!"

"You haven't seen my *ports de bras*... look! Tell me what you think."

She watched, very seriously. "I can't see anything wrong with them."

"That's cos I've been working on them. You probably don't need to. I bet yours are fine! You look like they would be."

A happy pink blush spread over her cheeks.

"Go on," I said. "Show me!"

I was right. Caitlyn didn't have arms like sausages! Not even Mum could have found anything to criticise.

"I think you're a natural," I said.

The pink blush turned slowly scarlet. "Really?" she said. She didn't say it like she was looking for praise; more like she truly valued my opinion.

"Not that it's ever easy," I said, "but some people just take to it. I mean, it helps, obviously, if you have a good teacher. I've been lucky. I've had a brilliant teacher right from the beginning. Mum's really strict, but she's the best!"

I paused.

"D'you want to do it again tomorrow?"

Her face lit up. "Could we?"

"I think we ought," I said. "I'm not going to rest until you can manage at least *one* decent pirouette! After that — well! We don't have to concentrate just on pirouettes; we can work on whatever you like."

"*Fouettés?*" she said breathlessly.

"Mm... maybe. I'm not quite sure you're ready for them. *She* hasn't got you doing them, has she?"

"No!" Caitlyn shook her head, quite vehemently. "I've just tried them out by myself."

"Oh, that's no good," I said. "You can't teach yourself. What about going on point? You haven't tried that, have you? Cos you're *certainly* not ready for that!"

Earnestly she said, "I wouldn't even think of it!"

"Well, that's a relief. You can cause permanent damage by going on point too early. Even I've only just started, and Mum still makes me stay at the barre. I'm longing to move away, but Mum is really strict. She says — oops!" I clapped a hand to my mouth as the big clock at the end of the gym suddenly made one of its loud clonking noises. I took one look and went, "Help, I'm supposed to be working on my choreography!"

"I'm sorry." Caitlyn sprang up. "I'll go!"

"You don't have to," I said. "You can always stay and watch."

"*Can* I?"

I said, "So long as you don't blame me if you get bored. I'm just trying stuff out."

"I won't get bored." She bounced herself on to the horse and settled there, cross-legged, like an elf. "I could sit and watch all day!"

Chapter Four

It was several days before Caitlyn finally trusted me enough to let me in on her secret. We'd taken to meeting up in the gym every morning, really early. First we'd do a bit of a warm-up, then I'd help Caitlyn work on some of the stuff that she was having problems with, and then, for the last half-hour, I'd try out my latest ideas for Miss Lucas and her dance interlude. Caitlyn would sit quiet as a mouse, on top of the horse, watching intently. Just as she'd promised, she never seemed to get bored.

I would have done! I would have got really twitchy, being forced just to sit and watch. I'd have been desperate to jump up and try things out for myself.

On the other hand it was true that some of the moves were obviously more advanced than Caitlyn could have tackled. I really *did* wonder who had been teaching her.

Occasionally my curiosity almost got the better of me so that I was tempted to start badgering her. But we were getting on so well! It would have seemed a shame to go and ruin everything. I found that I was really enjoying myself, taking her through all the basic steps that I'd been doing for years. Some she'd already got; others it was like no one had ever properly shown her.

I honestly never would have thought I'd have the patience to be a good teacher, but even when Caitlyn couldn't immediately master something I didn't click my tongue, or roll my eyes, or show that I was frustrated. I just gently — but firmly, cos you have to be firm — took her through it again. And yet again, if necessary, though it hardly ever was. She was extraordinarily quick at picking things up and, best of all, she didn't go backwards overnight. It drives Mum demented when she's spent ages teaching somebody how to do something and in their very next lesson they've gone and lost it. Caitlyn earnestly assured me that her *body* always remembered.

"I might have forgotten in my mind, but then when I start dancing my body just seems to take over."

I said, "Yes, that's good. It shows you have a dancer's instinct."

I wasn't sure if that was strictly true but she glowed when I said it. I know from experience that a bit of praise goes a long way. Mum hardly ever praises, and she specially doesn't praise me (cos of not wanting to be accused of favouritism) but on the rare occasions when she does I get this warm feeling inside me like melted chocolate.

I'd often wondered how Mum could bear being just a teacher after being a leading dancer, though Mum had always said that anyone who was *just* a teacher shouldn't be teaching.

"We owe it to future dancers to be the very best teachers we can."

She's always claimed it's deeply satisfying, but I'd never really believed her. Now, at last, I was beginning to do so. I felt so proud of Caitlyn – and of myself! – when she got the hang of something. I was sure I was a far better teacher than whoever it was she'd been going to. Maybe still *was* going to. But I was determined to bite my tongue and not push her. One day, hopefully, she'd feel ready to tell me, and until then I would do my best to be patient.

Just as well I wasn't put to the test for too long. Patience is a really difficult virtue! But one morning, quite suddenly, as we finished our warm-up, Caitlyn just blurted it out.

"You know you said you didn't think the person that was teaching me was up to it?"

I said, "Yes?" I didn't mean to pounce. But at last! Was she really going to tell me?

She took a deep breath. "There wasn't any person."

Oh, I thought, *not this again!*

"It was me."

I said, "*You?*"

She nodded and hung her head, like it was something to be ashamed of. I stared at her in disbelief.

"You've been teaching yourself?"

I'd never heard of anyone teaching themselves ballet! I didn't think you could.

Meekly she said, "I know I haven't made a very good job of it."

"But you have!" I said. "You've done a fantastic job."

She looked at me, uncertainly.

"Honestly! I only said about not being up to it when I thought you had a proper teacher. What's really incredible is you don't seem to have developed any bad habits. That," I assured her, "is just, like, totally amazing!"

"But I couldn't even learn how to focus properly!"

"No, cos there comes a point when you need help. You can't teach yourself *everything*. What I don't understand—" I hoisted myself up on to the horse and sat there, dangling my legs. "Since you've obviously got talent, and it's very, very wrong *ever* to waste talent, why aren't you having lessons?"

She didn't say anything to that; just perched beside me on the horse, her knees hugged up to her chin.

"You need to tell your mum, before it's too late! Or your dad," I added, not wanting to be sexist, though most of the dads I've met don't seem to be all that interested. My dad's different cos of having been a dancer himself. But it's always the mums, the pushy ballet mums, that Mum complains about.

"It's really important," I said, "to get started. Leave it any longer and it'll be too late!"

She heaved a sigh. "I know. I've wanted to learn for simply ages! Ages and ages! Ever since I saw *The Nutcracker*. I went with my school and I just loved it *so much*."

"So... why don't you have lessons?" I was at a loss. If she'd wanted to do it for so long—

"I can't!"

"But why not? Have you tried asking your mum? Or dad."

"I haven't got a dad. He died when I was a baby."

"Oh." That threw me. I couldn't think what to say. I'm not very good in these sorts of situation.

"It's all right," said Caitlyn. "I don't really remember him. But I can't ask Mum! It would upset her if she thought there was something I desperately wanted to do and she couldn't afford to let me do it. I know she couldn't cos she worries about money all the time."

"Suppose you told her you've got real talent? You could tell her that *I* said you had. You could say how I've been helping you and how I said you needed to start having lessons right away before it's too late. And then you—"

"I couldn't!" She shook her head, vehemently. "It would just worry her even more."

"But you're being held back! Surely she could manage

just *one* lesson a week? That wouldn't cost much! We could ask *my* mum. I bet she'd take you. Just once a week? I could still go on helping you. I really think you should ask her. I think you should do it tonight! Soon as you get back from school."

"I can't," said Caitlyn. "I *can't!*"

"Can't even ask for just one lesson a week?" I couldn't imagine anybody not being able to afford just one lesson. Nobody could be that broke! "Just *one lesson*," I said. "That's all you'd be asking for!"

She looked at me, tragically. "You don't understand."

"I don't think *you* do!" I probably said it a bit more sharply than I should have done. But all my life I've heard Mum saying how ballet is a precious gift and should be fed and nurtured. (Not quite sure what nurtured is. Taken care of, I *think*. Certainly not just tossed to one side cos of someone claiming their mum couldn't even afford one measly little lesson per week.)

"If you don't start with a proper teacher *right now*,"

I said, "you might just as well forget all about it cos it'll be too late."

She muttered, "Yes. I know."

"Well then, if you *know*—" I stared at her, exasperated. Why was she so stubborn?

Even as I watched, a tear rolled down her cheek, and then another, and another, until her eyes were brimming over. I thought, *Omigod, I'm behaving like Mum!*

"Look, I'm sorry," I said, "but there's no point pretending. If dancing really means anything to you, if it really, really means anything—"

"It means the whole world!" She sprang down off the horse. "But so does my mum!"

I was about to retort that if a person wanted to get anywhere as a dancer they had to be prepared to be totally single-minded and not be put off by anyone or anything, but at that moment the door opened and Miss Lucas appeared. It was probably just as well. Caitlyn was already quite upset enough without me making matters worse.

"Oh, girls!" chirped Miss Lucas. "You're still here! I'm glad you're so keen – you're obviously working extremely hard – but you do know the first bell has rung?"

We hadn't even heard it! Caitlyn, white-faced and miserable, was already halfway out of the door. I jumped down off the horse and set off after her.

"Do I take it," said Miss Lucas, "that you're getting on all right?"

I said, "Yes! Fine."

"Good! I'm very much looking forward to seeing the result – when you're ready, of course. Only when you're ready! I don't want you to feel under any pressure." She gave me an understanding beam. "I know you artists can't be rushed. I'm sure your dad doesn't like people hovering over him."

"Dad goes raving mad," I said. "He's very intolerant."

"Well, he's a gifted choreographer. He has every right to be."

I thought, *Tell that to Mum!* Not that Mum is the most tolerant person in the world. Sean once said that she and Dad were like a couple of hand grenades, ready to go off. *Not* what you would call comfortable people to have as parents. But of course I am quite proud to belong to them, and I have to admit it impresses people. Miss Lucas, for example. You'd think Mum and Dad were royalty, the way her voice goes all oozy.

"So, off you go," she said, making little *shooing* motions towards the door. "I don't want to be accused of making you late for lessons!"

I went on my way, feeling vaguely guilty. I hadn't done any work at all on her dance interlude that morning, I'd been too busy trying to bully Caitlyn. I could see, now, that I'd been a bit unkind. It's true it maddens me when people won't stick up for themselves, but being all pushy and upfront probably wasn't very helpful. Especially with someone like Caitlyn. I didn't want her going back in her shell and not talking to me again.

I managed to catch her while we were filing out of the hall after morning assembly.

"Please don't worry," I whispered. "We'll find a way around it!"

I would find a way around it. I am one of those people, I just refuse to be beaten.

I was considerably annoyed when we were back at our desks and Jordan, hissing like an angry wasp, demanded to know what I'd been whispering about. I felt like saying, "What's it to you?", but she probably felt she had a right to know. We weren't used to keeping secrets from each other.

"It wasn't anything very interesting," I said.

"So why whisper?"

"Cos we weren't supposed to be talking!"

"It's rude to whisper," said Livi. "I can't understand what you see in that girl. Someone said you were in the gym with her this morning. What was *she* doing there?"

I said, "Helping me, if you must know."

"What, *her*?"

"We're working on that thing for Miss Lucas."

"Why her? She's not a dancer!"

"Actually," I said, "as a matter of fact, she is."

Jordan snorted. "Doesn't look much like a dancer to me."

"She looks *exactly* like a dancer," I said.

I knew they were probably a bit jealous, and I could sort of sympathise cos of the three of us having been best friends for practically ever, but I had more important things to worry about than soothing ruffled feathers. There was a problem to be solved and it looked like I was the one who had to solve it.

I made a start that same evening, after class. I waited until Mum and I were back home by ourselves again, and Mum was relaxing with her glass of wine, then said, "You know that girl I was talking about? The one who said she didn't do ballet?"

"Not her again!" said Mum.

Well, at least she'd remembered who Caitlyn was. That was something.

"Turns out I was right," I said. "She does do it."

Mum said, "Ah. OK. Good."

"Just not with a teacher," I said.

"No?"

She wasn't listening properly! If she'd been listening properly, she'd have said, "How can someone do ballet without a teacher?" And then I would have explained. And then, maybe—

Then maybe Mum would sit up and take notice, like, "Do you want me to have a look at her?" Then Caitlyn could show Mum what she was capable of and Mum would be so impressed she would immediately offer her free lessons! Maybe.

"She's trying to teach herself," I said.

Mum gave a little snort of laughter. At last! I had got her attention.

"Do you suppose it's possible?" I said.

"No way," said Mum.

"That's what I thought! But honestly she's really talented. She hasn't developed *any* bad habits. Not as far as I can see. And I r—" I broke off at the sound of the front door opening.

"That'll be Sean," said Mum. "He said he'd be home early."

"Oh. Right. Well, like I was saying, I really—"

"In here!" called Mum.

"I really think sh—"

But already Mum had lost interest. What little she'd ever had. Sean is her big favourite. I don't really mind cos he's my favourite, too. He's everyone's! Mum says he has way too much charm for his own good. *And* he's better looking than anyone has a right to be. He takes after Dad, which is to say he has black hair and these really bright blue eyes, whereas me and Jen are more like Mum. Actually, to be honest, Jen is *very* like Mum. They are both redheads, green-eyed, with cheekbones to die for.

I am also a redhead, though more chestnut than Mum and Jen, and sadly I do not have cheekbones to die for. Mum says that my face is "distressingly round". Dad, trying to make me feel better, says that I am cheeky-looking. But who wants to be cheeky-looking? When they're hoping to dance all the great classics? *Swan Lake* and *Giselle* and *Sleeping Beauty*?

"Madeleine O'Brien made a cheeky-looking Giselle..."

I don't think so! I live in hope of growing thin and haggard as I get older. Never mind cheeky, I want cheekbones!

All the rest of the family have cheekbones. Life is very unfair. But not, I reminded myself, as unfair to me as it was to Caitlyn.

I said, "Honestly, Mum, I do think she needs to have proper lessons. I th—"

"Yes, yes," said Mum. "I hear you. How did this morning go?" she asked, as Sean came in.

"Yeah, fine. We're getting there." He was talking, I *think*, about the new production of *The Nutcracker* that the company were putting on. He saw me and raised a hand. "Hi, Beanie."

Don't ask! Just *do not ask*.

I said, "Have you got the evening off?"

"I have. If that's all right with you?"

"I s'pose they can manage without you," I said. And then, quickly turning back to Mum before she could lose track of what we'd been talking about, "See, if she doesn't have lessons *soon*—"

"Tell your brother," said Mum. "I'm going to make a cup of coffee."

I sighed.

"Tell me what?" said Sean, flinging himself down on the sofa.

I settled next to him, prepared for a cosy chat. Unlike Mum, Sean is someone who listens.

"It's this girl," I said. "This new girl. Caitlyn. She does *so* want to do ballet! She's been trying to teach herself, but—"

Sean groaned.

"No, she's good!" I said. "Really she is! It's just that her mum can't afford lessons and I'm worried about all that talent going to waste."

"So, what exactly were you proposing to do about it?"

Eagerly I said, "Well, I thought if I could just get Mum to take an interest—"

"*Get* her to take an interest? How do you ever *get* Mum to do anything?"

"I'd keep on at her," I said. "I'd just keep on and on until I wore her down!"

Sean shook his head. "Not a good idea. You'll need to be a lot more subtle than that."

I frowned. "How d'you mean?"

"I mean the only way you can ever hope to get Mum to do something she doesn't want to do is by letting her think it was her idea rather than yours."

"Oh." I crinkled my nose. "How would I do that?"

"Don't ask me! That's your problem."

"*You* could do it," I said.

"Why me?"

"Cos you're her favourite! She listens to you."

"But I don't know the girl! I don't know anything about her. Why this crusading zeal all of a sudden?"

"I'm just thinking how it's a crime to waste talent," I said. "That's what Mum's always telling us."

"Mum's always telling us lots of things."

"But what am I going to do?" I wailed. "I promised Caitlyn I'd solve the problem!"

"Shouldn't have done that," said Sean.

"Well, I did! And now I've got to. I thought if Mum saw her she might offer to teach her for free?"

"Oh, you poor deluded thing!" Sean reached out and ruffled my hair. I usually hate it when people do that. Sean gets away with things; he always has done.

"You're not being very helpful," I grumbled.

"If I could be, sweetheart, I would. I just don't see how I can help. Ah!" He sat up. "Coffee!"

Before I knew it, he and Mum were deep in company talk. Even though it's been years since Mum last danced, she's still keen to hear all the latest gossip. So am I, as a rule, but I was too bothered about Caitlyn and the promise I'd made. I could see, now, that I'd been a bit rash. Mum was too used to pushy ballet mums parading their untalented little darlings in front of her and expecting her to welcome them with cries of delight. It was a bit disappointing. I mean, I was *me*. I was her daughter! She should know by now that she could trust me. I wouldn't expect her to waste her time on some flat-footed pudding face of a girl. (Mum's words, not mine.)

I kept thinking of what Sean had said about letting Mum think it was her own idea. I couldn't immediately see how I was expected to make that happen, but I was already beginning to hatch a plan. Of sorts. If I could go on working with Caitlyn, even just for a short time every day, then perhaps by Christmas I'd feel she was ready to show Mum what she could do, and then *somehow* – though I wasn't at all sure how – I could get Mum to look at her. And once Mum saw for herself how talented she was – well! I couldn't believe she wouldn't offer to help.

I was on my way up to bed, later on, when Sean called after me.

"Hey, Bean! I've been thinking."

"Yes?" I spun around, hopefully.

"This girl you're so eager to help—"

"Caitlyn!"

"Did you say she went to your school? Because, if so, how come her parents—"

"Her mum," I said. "That's the problem! They're a one-parent family. They haven't got much money."

"Whatever! The question remains."

I said, "What question?"

"School fees?" said Sean

"Oh." I hadn't thought of that.

"It's obviously a question of priorities. On the one hand school fees – on the other ballet lessons. The mum plainly reckons it's more important to send her to Coombe House than to pay for her to learn ballet. Doesn't seem to me there's very much you can do about that. Sorry, kiddo!" He ruffled my hair again. "You can't fight everyone's battles."

Chapter Five

I knew that Sean was right. If Caitlyn's mum thought school fees were more important than ballet lessons, there wasn't very much that I could do about it. Not even if I went and explained how Caitlyn was talented and how talent shouldn't ever be wasted. My mum never seemed to listen to anything I said; why should Caitlyn's?

It was a bit disheartening, but I wasn't going to let it stop me. One way or another, Caitlyn was going to have lessons! After all, it was hardly her fault if her mum had her priorities wrong. I decided that just for the moment I would exercise what Mum calls *discretion*. Discretion is apparently something I don't have very much of. It means, as far as I can make out, not bombarding people with personal questions, no matter how much you might be dying to know the answers. I actually felt I deserved some answers, seeing as I was willing to give up my precious time to help her; though I supposed, to be fair, it was my choice. It wasn't like she'd asked me.

I couldn't understand, though, why her mum had chosen to send her to Coombe House. It's not as if it's a top school or anything. Mum always calls it tinpot. She only sent me there cos it's not very academic and means I can devote most of my energies to dancing and not have to cope with mounds of homework every night. But if, for instance, I'd wanted to be a brain surgeon or something, she'd have done better sending me to Shenley High. Why hadn't Caitlyn's mum sent *her* to Shenley High? Everyone says it's one of the best comprehensives in London. I couldn't understand it. It seemed the minute I'd solved one mystery about Caitlyn, another came popping up. But just for the moment, I reminded myself, I was going to be *discreet*.

Caitlyn wasn't there when I arrived at school early next morning. She came creeping into the gym a few minutes later, looking a bit uncertain, like maybe I was going to tell her I didn't want anything to do with her any more. I assured her that nothing had changed.

"I'll just go on teaching you until — well! Until I can find a better solution. But it's all right for now. I bet there are loads worse teachers than me!"

I didn't tell her that I was already hatching a plan. That somehow — even if I still didn't quite know how — I was determined on getting Mum to take notice of her. I just couldn't believe that Mum wouldn't be impressed! I couldn't *believe* she wouldn't offer Caitlyn free classes. Not the way she went on about how it was such a crime to waste talent. She went on about that almost as much as she went on about pudding-faced girls with legs like tree trunks.

At the end of our session, as we left the gym, I said, "I've got an idea! Why don't you come round after school one day and you can see the DVD Dad made of Mum when she was dancing?"

"Oh!" Her face lit up. "*Could* I?"

"Don't see any reason why not. Unless you live miles away, like Liv."

Livi had a really long journey every morning. She came by Tube – ten stops on the Jubilee Line! It meant I didn't very often see her out of school. It wasn't really practical for either of us to just drop by.

"We're in Old Church Lane," I said. "Where are you, exactly?"

I was surprised when she said "just the other side of the main road" cos that's the big estate, Coopers Field. I'd never met anyone from there before; it doesn't have a very good reputation. Caitlyn's cheeks had turned a bit pink. I immediately felt ashamed of myself. What did it matter where she lived?

"You're so lucky," I said. "That means you can walk

to school! *And* you're near the Tube. Sean would be so envious! He's always complaining about having to get the bus home after a performance. *Two* buses. The Tube would be so much easier. Specially when it's freezing cold or pouring with rain. Specially after you've been dancing all evening."

I was burbling, mindlessly.

"So, anyway," I said, "ask your mum! Ask her if you can come over next Monday. Monday's the best cos I don't have a class on Mondays." I didn't have classes on Tuesdays or Wednesdays, either. What was more important was that *Mum* didn't have classes on a Monday. It was her evening off, so she would almost certainly be at home. That meant I could introduce Caitlyn to her, and who knew? She might immediately think, *Oh! That girl is a dancer*, same as I had. At any rate, I thought, it was worth a try.

Caitlyn reported next day that her mum said it was fine for her to come and watch Dad's DVD, "So long as I'm home by five cos of it getting dark."

"No problem," I said. "The bus goes straight down the hill from our place to the main road. It only takes about ten minutes."

Or maybe I could get Mum to give her a lift, though on second thoughts it might be best not to tell Mum where Caitlyn lived. Not immediately, at any rate; not until she'd seen for herself how talented Caitlyn was. Mum gets these ideas into her head sometimes. She's convinced the whole of Coopers Field is inhabited by muggers and drug dealers. Sean laughs at her about it, Dad rolls his eyes and Jen goes, "Mum, for heaven's sake!" I am never quite sure what to think. I just hoped, for Caitlyn's sake, that Mum was wrong. I wouldn't like to think of Caitlyn living amongst muggers and drug dealers.

Mum was downstairs when we arrived home after school on Monday. Downstairs is the basement, where we eat and sometimes just lounge about.

I took Caitlyn down there and proudly presented her.

I said, "Mum, this is Caitlyn. She's come to watch your DVD that Dad made."

Mum said, "That old thing! What on earth do you want to show her that for?"

"Cos she's interested," I said. "She's—"

I was about to remind Mum who Caitlyn was – "She's the one I was telling you about!" – but right at that moment Mum's phone rang. Always something!

Mum mouthed at me across the room: "It's Jen! Do you want to get yourselves something to eat?"

We went back upstairs with some yoghurt and fruit and settled down to the DVD. We were about ten minutes in when Mum appeared.

"Maddy, I'm just popping over to Jen's for a bit. I'll be back in a couple of hours. OK? Nice to meet you, Caitlyn! Hope you're enjoying that DVD."

"I am," Caitlyn assured her, but Mum had already gone.

"Honestly, this house," I said. "Everybody always *going* somewhere. Why can't they just keep still?"

Five minutes later, Sean appeared. He popped his head around the door and said, "Hi, Beanie! Mum around?"

"No," I said, "she suddenly went rushing over to see Jen." And then, very quickly, before he could vanish: "This is Caitlyn. My friend from school."

Sean said, "Hi, Caitlyn!" He flashed her a dizzying smile and shot off into the house.

"Are you staying in?" I shouted.

"No! Due at the theatre."

I heaved a sigh. Wasn't *anyone* interested?

Caitlyn, bright pink from the effect of being smiled at, giggled in a slightly embarrassed way and said, "Why does he call you Beanie?"

"Oh, that's just him being silly," I said. "It's cos when Mum was having me she got one of those picture thingies they take when the baby's inside you—"

"A sonogram!" said Caitlyn, enchanted.

"Something like that." What was there to be enchanted about? Just because we were talking about my soppy brother? "Sean couldn't make out what it was supposed to be. He said it looked like a bean."

"They do, sort of," said Caitlyn. "My auntie had one."

"Yes, but he seemed to think Mum actually had a bean growing inside her... he was *eight years old*," I said. "Mum always says Sean keeps his brains in his feet."

"Like me," said Caitlyn; and then, covered in confusion, "I didn't mean... I mean, I just meant..."

"You remember things with your feet," I said, kindly.

Seconds later, Sean's head reappeared round the door.

"Did you say Mum had gone to Jen's? It's not the baby, is it?"

"You mean the bean," I said. Caitlyn giggled, and immediately clapped a hand to her mouth. "It's not due till the end of December."

"Oh, yeah. Right. OK, I'm off!"

"See what I mean?" I said. I tapped my head. "Brains in feet. Jenny's my sister, by the way. Mum's very angry with her."

"Really?" Caitlyn's eyes widened. "She didn't sound angry."

"No, but she is."

"Why? What's she angry about?"

"She doesn't believe in people having babies and giving up their career."

"But your mum had babies!"

"She didn't give up her career, though. Not till I was born and by then it was time for her to stop dancing, anyway. And as a matter of *fact*," I said, "it's me more than Mum who ought to be angry. If it wasn't for Jen, I'd be at ballet school by now. She was allowed to go when she was eleven. *I've* got to wait." It was a sore point with me. "Mum says she wants to make sure I know that it's what I really want to do. She thinks Jen wasn't dedicated enough. All that talent just wasted!"

"What about—" Caitlyn hesitated, then brought it out in a rush. "What about your brother?"

Her face had gone all pink again. She'd got it *really* bad. Too embarrassed even to say his name!

"Oh, well, Sean," I said. "He's Mum's favourite. He can get away with anything."

"So, when did he go to ballet school?"

"He waited till he was thirteen, but that was his own choice. I'm just dying to go! I'd have gone this term if only they'd let me."

"That means I wouldn't ever have met you," said Caitlyn.

"Well, not unless you somehow managed to have lessons and ended up as a dancer... It's such a small world, we'd be bound to meet sooner or later."

"Not if I didn't manage to have lessons."

"No..."

We both gazed for a while at the screen, where Mum was coming to the end of the mad scene in *Giselle*. I reminded myself, very firmly, that I was being discreet. No more questions! Not for the moment, anyway.

Caitlyn heaved a blissful sigh. "Your mum was so beautiful."

I said, "Yes, though Giselle wasn't ever really her best part. She was actually more suited to Queen of the Wilis. That's what Dad says."

Caitlyn heaved another sigh. "I dream about dancing Giselle."

"Yes." I nodded. "It's your sort of part. I'm more of a Swanilda."

"Oh, yes! I adore *Coppélia*! I can just see you as Swanilda... I love the bit where she's pretending to be a doll."

We both immediately sprang off the sofa and began jerking our arms and legs, humming the music as we did so.

"Is it something *you* dream about?" said Caitlyn. "Dancing Swanilda?"

"I don't exactly dream about it," I said. "It's more like I'm trying to be realistic. You have to face facts... I'm not really cut out to be a great classical dancer. I've got the wrong sort of face, for one thing. *And* the wrong personality. Like that day Miss Lucas had us all walking across imaginary tightropes? You took it seriously: I just wanted to make people laugh."

"Swanilda makes people laugh."

"That's why she's my sort of part. I'm never going to be like Mum."

Caitlyn looked at bit worried at that, as if she ought to be contradicting me, but couldn't quite bring herself to do so. She may not have had any proper training but even she could recognise that a distressingly round face, coupled with a loud, bouncing personality (*thank you very much, Dad!*), wasn't the most promising material for a future Giselle. Caitlyn would be perfect! I could just see her as the betrayed peasant girl, driven to her grave by grief and finding herself in the company of the dreaded Wilis, a vengeful band of spirits who had all been betrayed by their lovers. One of my favourite ballets, but no humour *at all*.

"Would you like to watch something else?" I said, as the DVD came to an end. "You don't need to go yet, there's bags of time. I'll walk you to the bus stop. No problem!"

"All right." She curled up happily on the sofa with her legs tucked beneath her.

"What shall we watch? We've got loads here! *The Rite of Spring*. Have you ever seen that? Or *Petrushka*, or—"

"What about the dance you're doing for Miss Lucas? You've never told me what the story is!"

"Oh, it's really yucky," I said. "It's all about this Christmas tree fairy that's got old and past it and these horrible, spoilt rich kids that chuck her out and get a new one and she's all, like, wet and cold and nobody wants her and—"

I gabbled through the story as fast as I could, expecting Caitlyn to join me in pulling faces. Instead, very seriously, she said, "So, where does your dance fit in?"

"Well, it's a sort of interlude halfway through."

"Before the fairy's rescued? While she's still lying in the gutter?"

"Yup." I nodded.

"So she's like... dreaming of when she was young?"

"Yup."

"And that's why she's doing all these pirouettes and *fouettés*?"

I was about to say *yup* for the third time and ask her if she'd like me to find a DVD with Sean in it, cos I knew she'd be too shy to ask for herself, when it struck me that a note of doubt had crept into her voice. Defensively I said, "I thought we needed a bit of excitement! Otherwise it's such a drag."

"It could be sort of touching," said Caitlyn.

I was silent a moment. "Are you saying you don't think it works, what I've done?"

"No!" She shook her head. "It's brilliant! It's just—" She hesitated. "I just thought maybe it might... break the mood?"

She said it almost apologetically, like who was she to criticise? Actually, just for a moment I did feel a flash of indignation. What did she know about dancing, compared with me? She who'd never had a ballet lesson in her life! Daring to tell *me* that I'd got something wrong. That was some nerve that was!

But then, quite suddenly, I was overcome with shame. *I* was the one at fault, not Caitlyn.

"You're right," I said. "It's totally out of place. It's just me showing off!"

Caitlyn bit her lip.

"It's OK," I said. "You're only telling me what I already know. I've known it all the time! I just didn't want to admit it. Here!" I pulled out the CD of the music I'd originally been going to use. "Tell me what you think of this."

Obediently Caitlyn settled herself into a listening position, eyes tight shut. I thought, *That's how Dad listens to music!* Dad always says that if he listens with his eyes shut he can see pictures in his head. Maybe it was the same for Caitlyn.

She sat right through, very still, without moving. If I'd asked Livi or Jordan to listen to anything classical, they'd have been sighing and fidgeting after the first few seconds. Not that I absolutely *had* to use anything classical; it just seemed more suited to the old-fashioned storyline.

"So, what do you think?" I said, as I took the CD out of the player.

"I think it's beautiful," said Caitlyn.

"Better than what I've been using?"

"Not *better*. Just..."

"More in the mood."

"Yes!" She sounded relieved. "More in the mood."

I said, "Hm."

"What is it? Is it something famous?"

"It's someone's *adagio*." I looked at the label. "Albinoni. I think it is quite famous, actually."

"It's kind of haunting," said Caitlyn. "And sad!"

I sighed. "It's what I should've used all along. I was going to! But then I thought maybe we needed something more exciting. Something –" I struggled for a moment – "something I could enjoy doing! I was thinking of me. Cos I've got this really strong technique?"

Caitlyn nodded, eagerly. "I know! I've watched you."

"But I'm not so good at *adage*. Like all the slow stuff?"

I didn't really have to explain to Caitlyn. She obviously knew almost as much about ballet as I did.

"Mum says it's where I'm weak. But that isn't any excuse," I said, sternly. "Just cos *I* think the storyline's a bit soppy."

"It isn't," said Caitlyn. "Honestly it isn't! It's really touching."

I pulled a face. "In that case my choreography ought to be touching. Otherwise I'm cheating." What was worse, I was letting Miss Lucas down. She trusted me, and all I was doing was seizing the opportunity to show how clever I was. "I'm going to have to start over!" I cried.

Caitlyn looked alarmed. "But you've done so much work."

"Yes, and it's all wrong! It's my own fault. I've been putting *me* above the show." Something Mum said you should never do. "OK!" I tossed the CD into my school bag, lying on a chair where I had slung it. "That's it! Tomorrow we start on something new."

"We?" said Caitlyn.

"Yes! We'll work on it together. I can't do it by myself," I said. I obviously could've done; I just felt that Caitlyn deserved to be included. After all, she was the one who'd finally forced me into admitting the truth.

Her cheeks had gone pink again – with pleasure this time. Like she couldn't quite believe that I was asking for her help.

I said, "I'll make up the steps and you can dance them so I can see what they look like."

She was practically crimson by now. I had never known anyone blush so much! I almost never blush at all, which probably means I'm not a very modest sort of person. Caitlyn was almost *too* modest.

"Really," I said, "it'll be fine! You're a Christmas tree

fairy who's too old and shabby to be put on top of the tree any more... I'm not going to expect anything too complicated. It's going to be sad and gentle and reduce everyone to tears!"

Chapter Six

"...step, step... into the arabesque... and... hold... and... step and... *demi-tour* and... that's it! Slowly, slowly she sinks down... she simply doesn't have the energy to carry on."

Caitlyn obediently crumpled, one leg tucked beneath her, the other extended, head drooping forward on to her knees, frail and exhausted: all hope gone.

I cried, "*Yes!* That's exactly how I want it!"

"Now your turn," said Caitlyn.

"I don't need to, I already know it!"

"*Please,*" she begged.

"I won't do it any better than you."

If as well, is what I privately thought. Caitlyn could

manage to look frail without any effort at all: I am the very picture of what Mum calls "rude health".

"Maddy, please," begged Caitlyn. "I love watching you dance!"

We were back at school after the half-term break. I'd finished sketching out Miss Lucas's dance sequence in the front hall at home. We have a really *big* hall, almost the size of a room in itself. Wasted space, according to Dad, but excellent for dancing, so long as the rest of the family isn't there. Dad, especially, would have found it impossible not to interfere and make comments.

Maddy, are you sure you want to do it like that?

If I could just offer a tiny suggestion?

The answer to which would be a firm no! This was *my* work – well, mine and Caitlyn's. It was true I was the one who had made up the steps, but she had inspired me. If it hadn't been for her, I'd still have been showing how clever I was, doing pirouettes and *fouettés* all over the place. I'd specially wanted to include a *pas de chat*. It was my favourite party piece just at the moment, very light and springy, like a cat. And I just happened to be good at it! But the Christmas tree fairy wasn't light and springy, she was old and sad and fragile, and I had Caitlyn to thank for reminding me.

"Everyone's going to weep buckets," she said, as I finished the sequence and sank down, trying my best to look frail.

To be honest, I still wasn't convinced I was doing it as well as Caitlyn. That is, *technically* I was. Technically I was way ahead of her. I do have a particularly strong technique. But I didn't have her line! I had to work at it: to her it was second nature.

"Let's run it just once more," I said. "I need to check the timing."

I was beginning to get a glimmer of how satisfying it was to see someone performing the steps that I'd made up. Just as I always used to wonder how Mum could possibly enjoy teaching, I had often puzzled how Dad could bear to give up dancing to concentrate on choreography. It always seemed to me that it must be really frustrating, specially as Dad spent half his time demonstrating how he wanted things done. Wouldn't he far prefer to be onstage himself?

Caitlyn said almost the same thing. "I don't know how you can bear to sit there and watch me! You do it so much better."

"I like to be able to see what it looks like," I said. "I can't see it if I'm doing it myself."

"But I was horrible! I wobbled when I did the arabesque. *You* didn't!"

"You won't, either," I said, "when you've had a bit more practice. We'll just go on working at it. You'll see! I bet by this time next week you'll be steady as a rock. You can't pick things up just overnight," I said. "Doesn't matter how talented you are. We'll go through it again tomorrow."

"OK." She nodded, eagerly, and seemed about to add something, then changed her mind. And then, quite suddenly, she changed it back again. "My mum was wondering, as I've been round your place, whether you'd like to come back with me on Monday and stay to tea?"

She brought it all out in one big gasp. I was quite surprised. I said, "Tea?"

"Well..." She faltered. "Only if you'd like to."

"I'd love to!" I said.

"Really?" Her face lit up. It was as if she'd half expected me to make some kind of excuse, just cos of where she lived. I didn't care where she lived! I was just curious to meet her mum and see what sort of person could possibly think school fees were more important than ballet lessons. It didn't make any sense!

"Monday would be fine," I said.

"That's what I thought," said Caitlyn. "Cos of you not having class. Oh, and you wouldn't have to worry about getting home afterwards. Mum said we'd take you. So d'you want to ask your mum if it's all right?"

"Oh, it'll be all right," I said. "Mum's very easy."

She was like some crazy mad person when she was teaching, striding up and down, smacking and poking at people, but in ordinary life she wasn't so bad. She mostly let us do what we liked, just so long as it didn't interfere with our dancing. All the same, I didn't actually breathe the dreaded words, *Coopers Field*. I just said, "We can walk there from school, and anyhow her mum's going to drive me back. Caitlyn," I added, "is the girl I've been telling you about."

"Yes, yes," said Mum. "I met her the other day. I do have a memory, you know!"

"Didn't you think she looked like a dancer?"

"To be honest, I didn't really notice," said Mum. "I agree she wasn't pudding-faced!"

"She doesn't have legs like tree trunks, either," I said.

Mum shook her head. "How could I be expected to know that when she was wearing trousers?"

I said, "Hm." I hadn't thought of that. I'd always reckoned our school uniform was quite cool, but maybe trousers did have their drawbacks.

"They could be hiding a multitude of sins," said Mum. "She could be bandy-legged, for all I know."

"Well, she's not," I said. It really is an uphill struggle, sometimes, with Mum.

I wasn't quite sure what to expect, going back with Caitlyn after school on Monday. I didn't really think we'd be mugged, in spite of the way Mum was always angsting about it, but I did worry a bit about gangs, and what it would be like inside one of the big tower blocks. Mum always said it must be like living in a coffin. She also said that the lifts smelt of sick and the stairs were covered in piles of dog mess. But maybe that was just Mum. As Sean pointed out, she'd never actually set foot inside a tower block. All the same, I was relieved when Caitlyn pointed to a cluster of little houses, with a patch of grass in front of them, and said, "That's where we are. We've even got a garden!"

She said it proudly, and I thought, *So much for Mum.*

"It's really not as bad as people make out," Caitlyn

assured me. "We're all just human beings. Not like we've got two heads or anything."

"Never thought you had," I said, but I felt a bit ashamed.

"Mum's ever so pleased you're coming," said Caitlyn. "She thought you might be too grand."

I said, "*Me?*"

"I told her who your mum and dad are. I showed her this book that's got pictures of your mum in it. She was well impressed! She doesn't actually know anything about ballet but she could see your mum's famous. You won't tell her anything about me, will you?" Caitlyn looked at me, anxiously. "You won't tell her you're giving me lessons? Cos it would worry her. She'd think it was charity and she won't accept charity."

"It's not charity," I said. "It's cos we're friends! And cos wasting talent is a crime."

"But you won't tell her? Will you? *Please!*"

Reluctantly I promised that I wouldn't, even though I'd been thinking that I might, if the opportunity arose.

But I didn't want to upset Caitlyn when she was so happy that I was going back with her.

"Mum'll still be at work," she said, as she let us into the house. "She doesn't get in till five. Soon as she's here we can have tea, and then we'll take you home cos I don't expect your mum will want you to be late. Look, this is my bedroom where I do my practice."

"In here?" I said. I couldn't help sounding surprised. Her bedroom was tiny!

Defensively she said, "I use the windowsill as a barre and I can check what I'm doing in the mirror. Over there." She pointed to a full-length mirror propped against the wall. "I found it one day... someone had thrown it out. So I brought it back home and cleaned it up and it's fine except for a few little marks. I can't imagine why anyone would've got rid of it. And look, there's the garden! Sometimes I practise out there. I know it's not perfect, but it's better than nothing."

I sank down on to the edge of her bed.

"How long have you been doing it?"

"Trying to teach myself ballet?" She sank down next to me. "Ever since I saw *Coppélia*... almost two years."

I shook my head. I couldn't believe how she had managed to teach herself anything at all. How had she known what to do?

As if reading my mind, Caitlyn said, "I've got all these ballet books." She waved a hand at a shelf above the bed. I twisted my head around to look at them. *Stars of the Ballet*, *Stories from the Ballet*, *Teach Yourself Ballet*, *Basic Ballet*, *Ballet for Beginners*, *Classical Ballet*, *The History of Ballet*...

"It's what I always ask for," said Caitlyn. "Ballet books! For Christmas and birthdays. I give Mum a list. And then sometimes I find them second-hand, like in charity shops or online. That's how I got the one with your mum in it. And DVDs! I've got some of those, too. Mum has this friend she works with. She's a huge ballet fan! She sometimes gives Mum stuff for me. Stuff she doesn't want any more. Mum says that me and Marje, we're obsessed."

"You're real balletomanes," I said. "But if your mum *knows*—"

Quickly Caitlyn said, "She thinks I just love watching it."

"You mean after all this time she hasn't realised what you're doing? Trying to teach yourself?"

"Well, she does, but... she thinks it's something I'll grow out of. Like when I was little I had this thing about collecting little china animals?"

"Collecting little china animals isn't the same as desperately trying to teach yourself ballet!" I retorted. And then, unable to contain myself any longer: "Can I ask you something? How come your mum would rather pay for you to go to Coombe House than have ballet lessons? I know that probably sounds a bit rude—"

"It does rather," agreed Caitlyn.

"Well, I'm sorry, but it's important! It could be ruining your whole life. And it's not like Coombe House is anywhere special. Mum once said it's quite tinpot."

"So why does she send you there?" said Caitlyn.

I pulled a face. "She wants me to be able to concentrate on my dancing. She reckons if I went to St Andrew's, the same as everyone else, I'd have loads more homework. I *wanted* to go to St Andrew's. All my friends from primary went there. I had the hugest battle with Mum! She let Sean go, but he always manages to get round her. It's sheer favouritism! She lets him do whatever he likes. *She* wanted him to go to Hallfield."

"Ooh, posh!" said Caitlyn. "Why didn't he want to?"

"Cos he's so *not* posh."

Caitlyn widened her eyes, like she didn't believe me.

"He gets on with everyone, like everyone gets on with him." I sighed. "It's just one of those things. You get used to it. He's totally spoilt."

Caitlyn giggled. "So are you!"

"How can you say that?" I stared at her, indignantly. "I'm not Mum's favourite!"

"No, but you are spoilt."

I frowned. "Is that why you didn't like me, when we first met?"

"I didn't *not* like you."

"But you were incredibly rude," I said. "When I asked you where you did ballet?"

"Yes." She hung her head. "I'm really sorry, I didn't mean to be so horrible. It was just... I've dreamt of being a dancer for so long, and all of a sudden there you were, with your mum, and your dad, and your brother, and how could I admit that I would've just *died* to have your chances?"

She tugged her hair out of its ponytail and shook it loose, like she was trying to hide her face.

"You know after I'd seen *Nutcracker* and I wanted more than anything on earth to have ballet lessons? The school I was at then, I had to walk past your mum's place every day. The Anderson Academy of Dance." She sighed. "I did so want to go there! But my gran had just died and Mum had to give up her job and go part time cos there wasn't anyone at home to look after me and I just knew it wasn't going to happen and there was this girl in my class who did ballet, and sometimes she'd bring her ballet shoes with her, all lovely and pink and satiny, and I did *soooo* envy her!"

"Did you envy me?" I said. "Did you resent me?"

"No! Well — maybe. Just a bit. Not cos you had lessons and I didn't, but cos you seemed to take it all for granted."

Quickly I said, "I don't if I stop to think about it. I know I've been lucky! But you still haven't told me why your mum thinks school fees are more important than ballet lessons?"

"It's not so much she thinks they're more important, just that she can't afford both. She worries so much about money!"

"So how come she m—" I was about to say, *How come she manages to pay for you to go to Coombe House,* but that sounded *really* rude. "Sorry," I mumbled.

"It's all right." Caitlyn pushed her hair back and sat up very straight, legs crossed, hands clasped in her lap. "When my gran died, she left this money to be used specially for my education."

"But ballet's education!"

"Yes, I know, but it's not what Gran would've wanted. She wanted me to go to Coombe House! She used to work there once upon a time, and she always told Mum it was her dream that I should go there. She thought it was such a lovely school!"

"Oh, well, of course it *is*," I said, desperately trying to remember what I'd said about it. I surely hadn't told Caitlyn that Mum referred to it as tinpot? "What did your gran teach?"

"She didn't teach," said Caitlyn. "She was a dinner lady. For years and years! She said the girls were all so polite and the teachers were really friendly. Not like where she was before, when they hardly even spoke to her. Not the teachers *or* the boys."

"Where was that?" I said. "Not Hallfield? Oh, I must tell Sean! He'll be so glad he didn't go there. He'd have talked to your gran all right! Sean talks to everybody."

"Even dinner ladies?" said Caitlyn.

"Everybody," I said. And then it occurred to me that

perhaps I'd sounded rather rude again. I didn't mean to! I'd just meant that Sean is really friendly and outgoing. Unlike Mum and Dad, who tend not to notice people unless they happen to be part of their own world.

"There's Mum!" Caitlyn bounced herself off the bed. "Let's go and have some tea. And *please*, Maddy, *please*! Remember what you promised?"

If you are rash enough to make a promise, you are duty-bound to keep it, but sometimes, I have to say, it is far from easy. In my head I'd rehearsed all the things that I would like to say to Caitlyn's mum if I ever met her. I'd planned to make these long, impassioned speeches about how it was a crime to waste talent. And then I would beg her and plead with her to give Caitlyn a chance.

"She needs to start lessons *now*, before it's too late!"

And I couldn't say any of it!

We had a proper sit-down tea, which we almost never have at home cos nobody's ever there, and Caitlyn's mum kept asking me the sort of questions that well-meaning grown-ups always ask when they want to show an interest, but can't quite think of what to talk about, like, "How do you get on at school, Maddy?" and "What's your favourite subject?" I didn't mind as I could see she was just trying to make me feel welcome, but Caitlyn kept shooting these agonised glances across the table, like she was just waiting for me to say something I shouldn't. And then her mum asked me the one that grown-ups always, *always* ask: "So, what are you planning to do when you leave school, Maddy?"

Caitlyn wailed, "*Mum!* She's going to be a dancer. I told you... all her family are dancers. Her mum, her dad, her brother, her s—"

"Yes, of course! I'm so sorry, Maddy." Caitlyn's mum smiled apologetically at me. "That was a silly question, wasn't it?"

"Well, not really," I said.

I couldn't help liking Caitlyn's mum, in spite of the terrible crime she was committing. She was small and pale, like Caitlyn, and seemed really anxious to make me feel at home. Unlike my Mum when I'd brought Caitlyn back with me. *My* mum had hardly even noticed she was there.

"Thing is," I said, "not everyone who comes from a ballet family goes on to become a dancer. Though I probably will," I added.

"Caitlyn's always said she wants to be a teacher. Haven't you?"

"I did once," said Caitlyn.

"Her gran would be so proud of her! It was her dream, you know, that she should go to Coombe House. Wasn't it?"

Caitlyn nodded.

"And now she's there and really enjoying herself. And all thanks to her gran!"

After we'd finished tea, Caitlyn said, "We probably ought to take Maddy home now, or her mum will start to worry."

She wouldn't, but I didn't say so. I could see that Caitlyn was growing increasingly uneasy in case I broke my promise. She needn't have been so anxious; even if I hadn't promised, I wouldn't have said anything. Her mum had been too nice! I could understand why Caitlyn didn't want to upset her.

I nearly did upset her, though. Or upset Caitlyn, cos I'm sure it would've done. When she'd said she and her mum would take me home, I'd automatically thought she meant they would drive me back. I was quite puzzled when we left the estate cos where did they keep their car? I was about to ask when Caitlyn cried, "There's the bus!" and went racing off to the bus stop, waving her hand.

It was then that I realised: taking me back meant putting me on the bus. Unless it meant actually coming on the bus with me?

It did! I couldn't believe it. Mum would never go to so much trouble! She'd just say, "Call a cab." *In spite* of having a car, which Caitlyn's mum obviously didn't. I tried telling her that she and Caitlyn really didn't have to come with me, it wasn't that dark, but she said she wouldn't hear of letting me go on my own.

"Whatever would your mum say?"

I didn't think, probably, that Mum would say anything. I was just glad that *I* hadn't said anything, like, *Oh, don't you have a car?* I squirmed with embarrassment just at the thought of it. Me and my big mouth! Except that for once I hadn't actually opened my big mouth. I felt quite proud of myself. I was learning!

Chapter Seven

One Friday when we were in the gym the door opened and Miss Lucas appeared.

"No, no!" She waved a hand. "Carry on, don't mind me."

"We were just warming up," I said.

"Quite right! I'll just sit quietly and watch."

Behind her back Caitlyn pulled an agonised face. *I didn't mind Miss Lucas watching, I never mind anybody watching me, but I could see it was embarrassing Caitlyn. She still wasn't really sure of herself.*

"Actually," I said, "we were just about to start rehearsing."

"Oh, good!" Miss Lucas settled herself comfortably on one of the benches. "That was what I was hoping. I don't mean to pry; I was just wondering how you were getting on?"

"Shall we show you?"

"If you would! That would be splendid."

I ran over to start the CD player. "Ready?" I said to Caitlyn.

She shook her head, vehemently, and hoisted herself up on to the horse. "You do it!"

I could have insisted, but I didn't want her doing anything she wasn't comfortable with. She *might* rise to the occasion – but, then again, she might not. I didn't really know her well enough yet to be certain, and I was scared it might destroy her confidence.

"Oh!" cried Miss Lucas, as the music began. "Albinoni's *Adagio*!" She clapped her hands. "An excellent choice!"

I reflected once again that if it hadn't been for Caitlyn I might still be using the first piece I'd chosen, all spiky and jazzy. I couldn't help wondering what Miss Lucas would have made of that.

As I reached the end of the sequence and sank down, frail and exhausted – I *could* be frail and exhausted! Dancers have to act as well as dance – Miss Lucas stood up and clasped her hands to her bosom. "Oh, Maddy," she said, "that was quite wonderful! *Exactly* what I was looking for. Thank you so much! Do you know, I was originally going to suggest some music that might be suitable? I'm so glad I didn't! I might have known I could trust you."

I said, "Well, but Caitlyn has helped. We've been working on it together."

"Wonderful! My thanks to both of you. I can't tell you how happy I am! Caitlyn, I shall make sure your name appears in the programme... *choreography by Madeleine O'Brien and Caitlyn Hughes.*"

I could see Caitlyn opening her mouth to protest. "Oh, but I really didn't—"

Quickly, I cut in. "Caitlyn's my understudy. She can

dance it as well as I can. So if I go and fall under a bus—"

"Oh, Maddy, please!" Miss Lucas looked horrified. "Don't joke about such things!"

"Well, you never know," I said. "That's how Mum got her first solo."

"Someone fell under a bus?" said Caitlyn, sounding shocked.

"No, they fell down some steps and broke their ankle."

Miss Lucas clicked her tongue, disapprovingly. "That's not going to happen here. But I'll tell you what, next year you must both do something. It's so nice, Maddy, that you've found a fellow dancer. I know last year you weren't very— well!" She put a finger to her lips. "Let us draw a veil. Best forgotten."

"What did she mean by that?" wondered Caitlyn, as Miss Lucas whisked herself away.

"Just that last year she wanted me to do something with this other girl, Poppy Johnson."

"The one in Year Eight?"

"The pudding face."

Caitlyn giggled.

"It was just *awful*. *Clump*, *clump*, *clump*, all over the stage. *And* she insisted on *pointe* work when she wasn't ready for it and kept wobbling and nearly falling over. *And* I got Mum to come watch and now Mum probably won't ever come to anything ever again!"

"By the way——" Miss Lucas's old grey head had appeared around the door again. "I meant to say... it's pouring with rain so we'll all be back up here for PE, but there's no need to pull that face, Maddy! I have something exciting lined up. Something I think you'll both enjoy."

"Not Greek dancing?" I said.

I know it was a bit cheeky, but I couldn't resist it. Fortunately Miss Lucas has a sense of humour.

"For that," she said, "you almost deserve Greek dancing! But no, this is something far more energetic.

★ 133 ☆

And just be warned... I shall expect some real performances from you two girls!"

I couldn't believe it when we all trooped up to the gym later on for PE and heard this really cool music coming from the CD player. Definitely not classical! We all exchanged wondering glances.

"Rock 'n' roll," said Miss Lucas, with a big beam. "And we are going to dance to it! Has anyone heard of a dance called the jitterbug?"

Slowly we shook our heads.

"Well, it was very popular in America in the 1930s. It was quite a craze! People were jitterbugging all over the place. It's a young person's dance; I'm far too old to demonstrate. If there were young men here, they'd be sweeping you up and swirling you round... upside down, over their shoulders, every which way. As there aren't, you will just have to make do."

Livi and Jordan gave loud groans.

"I know, I know," said Miss Lucas. "Life is very unfair.

Now, there are no set steps so it's entirely up to you what you choose to do. But lots of imagination, please! Listen to the music... be inspired. On your marks... get set, go!"

Within seconds everyone was jitterbugging like crazy all around the gym. I didn't have a chance to see what the others were doing, I was too bound up with the music. It was like having a big spring unwinding inside you, sending your arms and legs shooting in all different directions, at the same time as your hips were gyrating, your knees now knocking, now apart, your feet turning in and then out as you jerked to and fro across the floor. As different from classical ballet as could possibly be.

Afterwards Miss Lucas had us all dancing two at a time in front of the rest of the class. There was lots of movement, but watching with a critical eye (the way Mum had taught me) I could see that most people were just flinging themselves around without any real invention. Me and Caitlyn were kept till last and almost immediately we found ourselves dancing as a pair, mirroring each other's movements, coming together, breaking apart, following, circling, this way, that way. At the end there was a simply huge burst of applause, more than I'd ever had before.

"That was so fun," said Caitlyn. "Didn't you think so? Or was it—" She hesitated. "Was it something your mum would disapprove of?"

"Oh, Mum wouldn't disapprove," I said. "I mean, she'd probably whack me across the back of the legs if I tried turning my toes in during one of *her* classes—"

Caitlyn looked alarmed.

"It's what she does," I said. "She's like a maniac! She's always whacking people – or prodding them, or poking them. But she's not against other forms of dance. And anyway you know in *Rite of Spring*? They actually *do* dance with their toes turned in! Well, in Nijinsky's version they do."

"Really?" said Caitlyn.

"Like this." I demonstrated a few steps. "Haven't you ever seen it?" I had a sudden idea. "If you came round tomorrow afternoon, we could watch it and then you could stay to tea. It's only fair," I said. "You had *me* over for tea. Now it's my turn! Plus we could do some more glitterbugging, maybe."

Caitlyn giggled. "Jitterbugging!"

"Whatever." I waved a hand. "We could be the Glitter Girls! We could work out a whole sequence."

And maybe Mum would be there, and maybe she would stop to watch, and then *maybe*, at long last, she would see for herself that Caitlyn had real talent.

"Shall we do that?" I said.

Caitlyn nodded, blissfully. "Yes, please!"

"Come at about three o'clock," I said. Mum would almost certainly be home by then. "If you text me from the bus, I'll come and meet you."

Wouldn't you just know it? Mum wasn't yet back by the time Caitlyn arrived. She should have been! She finished her classes at half past two. Dad wasn't there, either. He'd come back from New York, but then gone whizzing off again, to Holland this time, which meant we had the house to ourselves. It was good, in a way. It meant we could glitterbug, as crazily as we liked, all over the hall. Caitlyn kept saying, "It's jitterbug, it's jitterbug!" But I thought that if there wasn't a dance called the glitterbug there ought to be, and we were inventing it.

I'd unearthed a rock 'n' roll CD and the music was pounding so loud, and we were flinging ourselves around so wildly, that we didn't immediately realise we were being watched. Not until a familiar voice said, "What's all this, then?"

It was Sean and his friend Danny. They must have been downstairs.

"We're glitterbugging!" I cried.

Caitlyn didn't correct me. She'd either given up the unequal struggle (as Dad is fond of saying) or she'd been struck dumb. Struck dumb was my guess.

I did a knock-kneed zigzag towards her, daring her to stop.

"Yes, carry on, carry on! Let's all have a go!"

Before I knew it, Sean had sprung forward. He never can resist the temptation to join in! Very soon we were all three glitterbugging to and fro across the hall. *If there were young men here*, Miss Lucas had said, *...they would be sweeping you up and swirling you round... upside down, over their shoulders, every which way.*

Jordan and Livi would have been so jealous! Sean is only my brother so I am quite used to dancing with him, he doesn't overwhelm *me*; but Caitlyn confessed later on, a *lot* later on, that it had made her go "all funny".

Danny, meanwhile, had got his camera out and was snapping away as fast as he could go.

"Don't worry," he assured us. "I won't use anything without your permission."

"Why would he want to use our photos?" Caitlyn

wondered, when Sean and Danny had gone wandering off to another part of the house, leaving us on our own.

"Cos he's a photographer," I said. "He does photos of the ballet — well, and other things, too, but ballet's what he most loves. He's Sean's boyfriend," I added.

I don't quite know why I added that. I didn't do it on purpose to see if it would make her blush; it just seemed like a normal bit of conversation. Like if Jen and Steve had been there, I'd have said, "Steve is Jen's husband." But it was enough just to mention Sean's name to turn her bright pink. She obviously had a massive crush on him!

"We thought for a bit," I said, "he was going out with this girl in the company who's a real prima donna. Really pushy. Always reaching out and grabbing. Just *me, me, me*! It's one thing," I said, "to seize every opportunity, but that doesn't mean trampling all over everybody else. I mean, *I'm* quite pushy, but I wouldn't ever trample."

I was only burbling on to give her a chance to turn a bit less pink. I am *so glad* I don't blush!

"Danny's really nice," I said. "Mum says he's a good influence cos he's older than Sean and he's got more sense. I think our glitterbugging went really well, don't you? I might ask Dad if he could do a glitterbug ballet. Or we could do one! Just for ourselves. We could call ourselves the Glitter Girls. Hey, Sean!" I yelled. "We're the Glitter Girls! D'you want to do some more?"

"Sorry, can't," said Sean. "Just going to grab something to eat then set off."

I sighed. Everybody always coming and going! And where was Mum?

"Did you specially want her?" said Sean, as we all trooped down to the basement in search of food.

"Not particularly," I said. I *had*, but it was a bit late now. "Thing is it's going to be dark soon and I don't know how Caitlyn's supposed to get home."

"It's all right," whispered Caitlyn. "I can take the bus."

Crossly I said, "No, you can't! You didn't let me come home by myself."

"Where do you live?" said Sean.

"She lives just near school," I said. "Coopers Field."

I watched carefully for any reaction, but Sean isn't like Mum. It doesn't bother him where people live.

"No problem," he said. "We can take her. Right?"

He glanced at Danny, who said, "Sure."

"We'll get the bus down there then we can hop on the Tube. All settled! OK?"

Caitlyn tugged urgently at my sleeve. "Honestly," she whispered, "they don't have to."

"Well, they're going to," I said. "It's what brothers do."

It was what mums ought to do, if ever they were there. Or dads, if they weren't always racing to and fro.

Caitlyn went off at six o'clock, blushing furiously, with Sean and Danny. Mum arrived five minutes later.

"Sorry, sorry!" she said. "I got held up. Did you find something to eat?"

"Me and Caitlyn did," I said.

"Oh!" Mum stared around, as if Caitlyn might be hiding somewhere. "Is she still here?"

"No, Sean and Danny took her home."

"That was nice of them."

"Well, someone had to," I said. "Her mum doesn't like her being out in the dark. I thought you were going to be here! She came for tea, but we were all by ourselves. Why is everybody always *out* somewhere? When I went round to her place, her mum was there and we all sat down together, at a *table*, cos it's what people do. When people come to tea, they all sit down. They *talk*. Caitlyn must think we're a really weird family!"

"Oh, dear," said Mum. She sounded faintly surprised, as if such a thing had never occurred to her. "Do you honestly think so?"

"There's never anybody around," I said. "Dad's always away, and you're always busy, and Sean just stays long enough to say hallo and—"

"He uses the place like a hotel," said Mum. "He might

just as well move in with Danny and be done with it. As for your dad, you know he's in huge demand, and I can't just ignore these pushy mothers with their pudding-faced daughters always wanting me to tell them how brilliant they are. I only wish I could! But I'll tell you what, why don't you ask Cathleen—"

"Caitlyn!" I snapped.

"Caitlyn. Ask her over next Saturday and I promise I'll be here and we'll all go and sit down together and have tea and talk. And who knows? Your dad should be back, and Sean will probably look in, and she's probably got a thing about him, because all your little friends seem to, so that should make you happy."

"Why should it make me happy?" I said. "I haven't got a thing about him."

"It will make *her* happy."

I thought that in all probability it would just make her tongue-tied.

* * *

I asked Sean, next day, if he and Danny had dropped Caitlyn off OK. He said, "Of course we dropped her off OK! What do you take us for? You think we'd just abandon her? We even waited till she was safely indoors."

"Thank you," I said. "That was very kind of you."

"I am very kind."

"You're both very kind!"

"Well, I'm sure Danny will be glad to know you're grateful. It was an uphill struggle getting her to talk. She hardly said a word from start to finish. You didn't tell me she was so shy."

"She's not shy," I said. "She's just got this monstrous great crush on you."

"Really?"

I said, "Yes, really! Don't look all puzzled; you should be used to it by now."

He must surely have realised? Caitlyn couldn't have made it more obvious! But now that he was aware I knew I could trust him to be gentle and not tease. In spite of being so horribly spoilt, Sean is actually quite an understanding sort of person.

"So, what did you think of our glitterbugging?" I said. "What did you think of Caitlyn?"

"She's a nice little mover," said Sean, "but I don't think it was really her sort of thing. It's your sort of thing, it's even my sort of thing, but she strikes me as being more sylph than Glitter Girl."

"Yes." I nodded. Sean had seen it! "I'm teaching her the dance I'm doing for the Christmas show."

"I hope it's not going to be like last year!"

I flushed. "That wasn't my fault. Miss Lucas made me use some horrible pudding face who couldn't dance. This year it's just me. It's going to be very sad and touching."

"You reckon?" Sean laughed. "I can't see you being sad and touching!"

"I can be," I retorted.

"Show me?"

Well! I never need to be asked twice.

"This is just the first couple of minutes," I said.

"So what music are you using?"

"A thing called Albinoni's *Adagio*."

"OK! Off you go. I'll hum, you dance."

"You know it?" I said.

"Oh, please!" said Sean. "I know everything. Get on with it!"

I didn't do the whole sequence cos, even in the empty space of the hall, there really wasn't enough room, but I did it as sadly and touchingly as I possibly could. Sean may not be as withering as Mum but he is just as critical.

"So?" I said, hopefully. "What do you think?"

"You're right," said Sean. "It is sad and touching. I'm impressed!"

I preened. I couldn't help it!

"Mind you," he continued, going and ruining it all, "that probably *is* more your little friend's sort of thing. It would suit her down to the ground."

That got me a bit miffed. It might have been what I'd already thought, but I didn't need Sean telling me.

"Caitlyn's not a dancer," I said, huffily.

"Excuse me? Just the other day you were doing your best to convince me that she was!"

I said, "Well, she is and she isn't, if you see what I mean."

"Not really."

Still rather cross I said, "She *would* be, if someone would just give her a chance! I'm doing my best, but I can't do everything. I'm not a teacher! If Mum would just give her a scholarship or something..."

"Mum doesn't do scholarships."

"Well, free classes!"

"Be fair — she's not running a charity. She's running a business! If she gave free classes to every pudding face that can't afford to pay..."

I said, "Caitlyn's not a pudding face! And, while I think of it, could you let me have a signed photo for her? And could you put 'With love from Sean'? *Please?* Sean? Pretty please!"

"Don't grovel," said Sean. "It doesn't suit you."

"Well, but could you? It would so make her day!"

He groaned, but he let me have the photo, signed the way I'd asked. I knew he would! I can always get round him. And it was worth doing a bit of grovelling just to see the way Caitlyn's face lit up when I gave it to her.

I said, "Oh! You look like Clara in the Kingdom of Sweets!" I clasped my hands and made my eyes go big. "It's only *Sean*," I said.

Livi and Jordan had obviously been listening as hard as they could go cos Livi came up to me later and said, "Who's Clara?"

"In *The Nutcracker*," I said. "When she sees the Prince."

"So, what was all that about Sean?"

"Nothing! I was just giving Caitlyn his photograph."

"You were giving her Sean's photograph?" They stared at me, accusingly.

"You never gave us his photograph," said Jordan.

"No, cos you're not into ballet," I said.

"Doesn't mean we wouldn't like a photo."

"Could at least have offered."

 149 ☆

I said, "Well, but... if you're not into ballet, why would you want one?"

Livi tossed her head. "Don't have to be into ballet," she said.

"It's the principle," said Jordan. She linked her arm through Livi's. "We obviously don't count!"

They went stalking off together, noses in the air. I had the uncomfortable feeling that it was the end of our friendship. I'd known Livi and Jordan for years, Caitlyn for just a few weeks. Was I being disloyal?

I thought I probably was, but Caitlyn and I had so much in common! Plus I'd be off to ballet school full time as soon as I turned thirteen so we'd probably lose touch, anyway.

All the same, I couldn't help feeling a bit sad. It's never nice to fall out with your friends.

Life is just *so* difficult at times.

Chapter Eight

"Ha, tea!" cried Dad. "Real sit-down tea! What's brought this on all of a sudden?"

I said, "Da-a-a-d!"

I didn't want Caitlyn thinking we'd made a special effort just for her. I mean, we *had*, but she would find it embarrassing. I could see she was already a bit overwhelmed, what with everybody being there. There was Dad, there was Mum, there were Sean and Danny, and even Jen, hugely pregnant and looking like a beach ball. I knew Caitlyn wouldn't have any trouble talking to Jen, and I really thought that by now she ought to be able to cope with Sean and Danny, specially as they'd seen her home the other night. They're not in the least bit scary and I'd never known anyone be shy with Sean for very long. Not even when they *did* have a massive crush on him. Mum and Dad, on the other hand, are a different matter. Jordan once gigglingly said that they were a bit like royalty.

I'm used to them, of course, but even I can see that they are rather overwhelming. Dad in particular. He was once described in a dance magazine as one of the leading figures of British ballet and I do sometimes think he finds it difficult to just relax and be a normal, ordinary dad. Mum at least *tries* to be a normal, ordinary mum, except when she gets carried away in the studio, poking at people and reducing all the pudding faces to tears. She'd really made an effort with tea, even if she still couldn't get Caitlyn's name right.

"Cathleen," she said, pushing a plate towards her, "just dive in! Please!"

"Mum, it's Caitlyn," I said.

"Sorry, sorry!" Mum beat a fist against her forehead.

"Memory's going! But then I've never been good with names."

"Caitlyn's nice," said Jen.

I leaned forward earnestly across the table.

"Caitlyn," I said, "w—"

I was about to say, "wants to be a dancer". Followed by, "Unfortunately her mum can't afford lessons." And then perhaps, "I'm trying to teach her myself. She's really talented!"

This would at once rouse Jen's interest cos how could it not? It might even arouse Dad's, if he was listening, which he almost certainly wasn't, but I didn't need Dad. Jen would do! She would immediately see the unfairness of it. I saw her turning to Mum and going, "Oh, that is *so* tragic! Maybe you could give her a scholarship?"

It was on the tip of my tongue – and then Danny went and jumped in and the moment was gone.

"So, have you chosen a name yet?" he said.

He meant, *of course*, a name for the baby. Like anyone

cared! Well, Jen obviously did. And Mum and Dad, I suppose. Maybe Sean. Maybe, perhaps even me; just a little bit. But why, why did he have to go and ask at that particular moment?

Jen, needless to say, couldn't wait to get started.

"Well, if it's a boy," she said, "we thought of James. Either James or Ivor. I like James, Steve likes Ivor. If it's a girl, we both want Anya. We're waiting to see what turns up!"

"They're waiting to see if it's a girl bean or a boy bean," I said.

Sean pulled a face at me across the table. "That's enough from you, smart mouth!"

"So you haven't gone for one of those picture things?" said Danny.

"You mean a beanograph," I told him.

"A what?" said Danny.

I said, "Beanograph! Ask Sean! He knows."

Sean made his fingers into a gun shape and pointed them at me.

"You're not allowed to do that," I said. "It's not PC. Tell Danny why you call me Bean!"

"Yes, do," said Danny. "Is it a family secret?"

"It's Sean keeping his brains in his feet," I said.

"The best place for them," said Sean. He pushed back his chair. "Mum, we've got to go. We only looked in to say hallo. Bye, Jen! Bye, Glitter Girls!"

"What's this about Glitter Girls?" said Mum, as Sean and Danny disappeared up the basement steps.

Eagerly, I told her. "It's a dance we made up from what they used to do in America... the glitterbug. Well, ours is the glitterbug. Theirs was the jitterbug, but I think glitterbug's better. D'you want to see?"

I was all set to jump up and demonstrate, but Caitlyn plucked anxiously at me.

"Maddy, we're still working on it!"

"Doesn't matter," I said. "We can show them what we've done so far. It's only Mum and Dad! You don't have to be shy."

Of course it was the very *worst* thing I could have

said. I realised that the moment I'd said it. *Only Mum and Dad...* Caitlyn gave me this look like a drowning puppy. Mum, quite sharply, said, "Maddy, don't be so bossy! If *you* want to show off, by all means do so, but stop trying to force Caitlyn into it. She's a guest in this house! We don't make our guests feel uncomfortable."

Well! That probably just made her feel even more uncomfortable. It made *me* just feel cross. Partly cross with Caitlyn for being such a wimp, but even crosser with Mum for not supporting me. If she could only have been a bit encouraging, like, *Yes, come on, give us a demonstration*, instead of wittering on about not making our guests feel uncomfortable, I felt sure I could've got Caitlyn dancing. And then they would *all* have seen what she could do! Dad and Jen, as well as Mum.

Caitlyn obviously knew that I wasn't pleased. She plucked nervously at my sleeve as we went upstairs to my room after we'd finished tea. I said, "*What?*"

"I couldn't," she whispered. "I just couldn't!"

"That was an *opportunity*," I said. "And now you've gone and wasted it."

"But it was your mum," she pleaded. "And your dad!"

"Like I said... an opportunity! You have to *take* opportunities."

She bit her lip. "I just didn't think I was ready."

"Of course you were ready! It's not like learning —" I waved a hand — "I don't know! The Sugar Plum Fairy or something. There aren't any *set steps*. It's something you can just make up as you go, like we did for Miss Lucas. Like we did the other day, when Sean and Danny walked in. You didn't get all silly about it then!"

"That's cos I was in the middle of it."

"It was cos you're a *dancer*. Brains in your feet! Even if you get all woozy cos it's Sean and you've got a crush on him, your feet still keep on dancing."

Caitlyn's face was already starting to grow pink. It was the only time she had any colour, when she was embarrassed. She didn't bother trying to deny that she had a crush. Wouldn't have been any point, anyway, cos I wouldn't have believed her.

"If you can dance in front of Sean, you can dance in front of Mum," I said.

I knew I was being unkind cos nobody, but nobody, could ever be scared of Sean, I shouldn't think. Mum, on the other hand, strikes terror into all kinds of people.

"Thing is," I said, "if you want to get anywhere, you have to make an effort. You have to be prepared to push yourself. I don't mean trample over everyone like that girl I was telling you about, the one we thought Sean was going out with, cos she's just horrible and everybody hates her. But it's no use getting all embarrassed and hiding in the corner, cos that way no one's ever going to notice you. They'll never even know you're there! And loads of people that haven't got half your talent will just grab all the limelight and you'll still be stuck in the corner and you won't have anybody to blame except yourself! Cos nobody," I said, "can do it for you."

She hung her head. "I know. It's up to me."

"Well, it is! I'm doing my best," I said. "I can't do more. And I can't do it all by myself! You've got to play your part, otherwise it's not fair." I really felt that it wasn't. I'd tried so hard to create opportunities! I'd spoken to Sean; I'd spoken to Mum; I'd given Caitlyn lessons. What more was I expected to do?

"By rights," I said, "I ought to drag you back downstairs and *make* you dance the glitterbug whether you like it or not!"

She shrank back. "Maddy, please—"

"Oh, don't worry," I said. "I'm not actually going to do it. I would if I were Mum. Mum never takes no for an answer! She'd make you, and then we'd know for sure whether you've got what it takes or whether you're someone who just goes to pieces."

Tears sprang to her eyes. "I might be someone who just goes to pieces."

"No, you wouldn't," I said. I felt, too late, that I'd been a bit harsh. I hadn't meant to make her cry! I know I can be bossy, but it was just *so* frustrating. "People like you and Sean," I said, "people who keep their brains in their feet, you never go to pieces. You're the lucky ones!"

She blotted her eyes with the back of her hand. "What about you?"

"Oh! Well. Me." I didn't honestly think that I would go to pieces, either, but right now I needed to comfort her. "I'd just... I don't know! Carry on, I suppose, and make an idiot of myself."

"I don't think you'd ever make an idiot of yourself," said Caitlyn.

"No, and neither would you! You've got to have *confidence*," I told her.

"But in front of your mum and dad!"

I couldn't very well say *what's so special about Mum and Dad* when even Livi and Jordan thought they behaved like royalty.

"Maybe they are a bit scary," I agreed. "But you know what?"

"W-what?"

"D'you want me to tell you what Sean said after *he* saw you dancing? He said you were *a nice little mover*. And if Sean thinks you're a nice little mover then Mum and Dad would, too! So that means it was a whole wasted opportunity. You can't *afford* to waste opportunities."

I was bullying again! The tears had already sprung back into her eyes. I knew it was unfair of me, when my life had been nothing but one massive great opportunity from the very beginning, while Caitlyn hadn't had any opportunities of any kind whatsoever. But she was going to have to push herself forward a bit or she simply wouldn't stand a chance.

"Let's not talk about it any more," I said. "Let's watch something! Tell me what you'd like to see and I'll go downstairs and get it. Dad has DVDs of practically every ballet ever written – and every dancer that's ever danced in them. Would you like to see *Swan Lake* with Jen being a Little Swan? Sean's there somewhere as well, but it was before he became a soloist so whatever you do don't blink or you'll miss him!"

"I won't," said Caitlyn. "I won't!"

"That's right," I said, "cos you wouldn't want to miss *Sean*!"

She managed a little wobbly smile; she knew I was only teasing. All the same, I think we were both glad at seven o'clock when Steve arrived to pick up Jen and offered to give Caitlyn a lift home. It wasn't a school night so she could have stayed later, but she was still a bit wary, like she was scared I might start on at her again. I wouldn't have done, cos I wasn't cross any more. I have the sort of temper that flares up really fast, almost before I know it's happening, and then suddenly dies down just as quickly. I never bear grudges. On the other hand I did have questions I wanted to explore, like how long she could carry on with just me teaching her and whether, without realising it, I might be letting her get into the sort of bad habits that Mum would never tolerate? I kept remembering what Sean had said.

The only way you can ever hope to get Mum to do something she doesn't want to do is by letting her think it was her idea rather than yours.

But how? How was I supposed to do that? I knew it wasn't any use nagging. Mum reacts really badly when she's nagged. And Dad was hardly ever there and even when he was he was far too busy to bother himself with little unimportant things such as Caitlyn not being able to have ballet lessons. Jen obviously wasn't any use. All *she* could think about was the baby. And I'd already tried Sean. What else could I do? There had to be something!

Monday morning, when we met up in the gym, Caitlyn immediately burst into apologies.

"Maddy, I'm really sorry for the way I behaved! You're trying so hard to help me and I just let you down! If you don't want to have anything more to do with me, I'll understand, cos I really don't deserve it and—"

I had to stop her. I said, "You surely don't think I'd give up on you now? After all the hard work we've put in!"

"But I'm just so *stupid*!"

"Actually," I said, "you're not. It's me that's stupid."

Her eyes widened. "*You?*"

"Yes! Trying to rush things."

I'd been having lots of thoughts over the rest of the weekend. I'd been going back over what Sean had said.

She's a nice little mover, he'd said, *but I don't think it was really her sort of thing.*

It was my sort of thing, it was Sean's sort of thing; but not Caitlyn's.

She strikes me as being more sylph than Glitter Girl.

Which meant that maybe Caitlyn had been right all along and it would've done her no good at all if I'd made her show Mum our glitterbug dance.

I was remembering, as well, another thing that Sean had said. It was after seeing my Christmas tree fairy dance. He'd said that that probably *was* more Caitlyn's sort of thing; *it would suit her down to the ground.*

I'd been a bit miffed at the time. My own brother as good as telling me that *my* dance that *I'd* made up would suit Caitlyn more than it suited me! Of course I'd known that he was right; I just didn't like being told.

But now I was thinking back and I couldn't help feeling hugely relieved that Caitlyn's instinct had obviously been better than mine. I might have gone and ruined everything for her!

She was looking at me like I'd just trampled all over her dreams and ground them into dust.

"You mean..." She had to swallow and start again. "You mean I'm just not good enough!"

Very quickly, cos I didn't want her going all to pieces, I said, "No! That wasn't what I meant at all. It's not your dancing that's the problem, it's you not trusting yourself!"

It must be truly terrible, I thought, *to have so little confidence*. Me, I have masses of it! Too much, Mum sometimes says, for my own good. Sean's the same. We are just naturally very confident sort of people.

Even when Mum criticises me in front of the whole class, like, "Maddy, for goodness' sake! You're not training to be a heavyweight wrestler!" it doesn't really put a dent in my confidence. It certainly doesn't reduce me to tears like it does some of the others. If anything, it just makes me defiant. (It also makes me determined to do better, if only to show Mum.)

Caitlyn was really quite fragile. If Mum yelled at her like she yelled at me, she would be utterly crushed. But then, I thought, Mum probably wouldn't yell at Caitlyn. She only ever yelled at people who could take it.

"Listen," I said to Caitlyn, "it's not the end of the world. There'll be other chances! What we're going to do, we're going to keep on as we are until – well! Until I find a solution. Cos I will find one! *I'm* not going to give up and I'm not going to let you, either. If you ever even think of it," I threatened, "I shall never speak to you again!"

That evening I cornered Mum in the kitchen while she was making a cup of coffee and couldn't escape. I said, "You are going to come to the end-of-term show, aren't you?"

"Am I?" said Mum. And then, "All right, all right, only joking! I can't really say no, can I?"

I agreed, rather sternly, that she couldn't. "Miss Lucas would be ever so disappointed if you weren't there."

"Yes." Mum sighed. "I know. You'd better get me a ticket."

"Just the one?"

"Well, your dad won't be here, he'll be in Australia, Sean's bound to be dancing and Jen won't be in a fit state, so – yes! Just one."

"I think this year you might quite enjoy it," I said.

"I doubt it," said Mum. "Miss Lucas is a sweet old dear and I'd never do anything to hurt her, but after last year—"

I assured her that it wouldn't be like last year. I reminded her that Miss Lucas had left all the dancing stuff to me. I'd chosen the music, I'd done the choreography. Miss Lucas hadn't had anything to do with it.

"And you absolutely promise me no pudding faces?" said Mum.

"No! Just me."

"In that case it had better be worth watching."

"It is," I said. "I let Sean see and he said he was impressed."

"Really?" For the first time Mum showed a flicker of interest. She always says that even if he does keep his brains in his feet and has lousy taste when it comes to women (like the hideous, pushy creature we'd thought he was going out with) you can always rely on his judgement when it comes to dancing. It was just a pity,

I thought bitterly, that she couldn't rely on *my* judgement.
I'm sure I'm every bit as reliable as Sean!

"OK, get me a ticket," said Mum. "But be warned...
I shall expect something special!"

Chapter Nine

At last! I had a plan. Sort of a plan. There was definitely something buzzing about inside my head. I knew what I wanted to do: I just hadn't quite worked out how to do it.

I'd made sure Mum was going to be there; that was the most important thing. If Mum wasn't there, it would all just be a wasted effort. Next step was impressing upon Caitlyn that she *really was* my understudy, and that understudies have to be prepared to go on at a moment's notice.

She giggled when I said that. She thought I was joking!

"I'm serious," I said. "There's no point being an

understudy if you're not ready to go on. *Are* you ready to go on?"

That stopped her giggling. She looked at me, worried.

"Why would I have to go on?"

"Cos you never know what might happen," I said. "Your big chance could come at absolutely any moment! Like when Mum took over as the Lilac Fairy? She'd just been an ordinary member of the corps de ballet then *wham!* All of a sudden she's dancing a solo."

"D'you think she was scared?" said Caitlyn.

"Oh, probably," I said, though it was hard to imagine Mum ever being scared of anything. I don't think I would be; not so long as I'd learnt the part properly. I'd be excited!

"I'd be terrified," said Caitlyn.

"No, you wouldn't," I said. "I've told you before... brains in your feet! They'd just take over."

She looked so doubtful that for a moment I wondered

if my plan — my sort of a plan — might not be such a brilliant idea. But you have to be prepared to take a chance!

"Tomorrow," I said, "we'll have our own private dress rehearsal and you can dance so that I can see if things are working out."

Caitlyn didn't mind dancing in front of me. To begin with she'd been embarrassed and it had made her nervous and uncertain, but she was used to it by now. Of course, I wasn't Mum...

"Was that all right?" she asked, anxiously.

I told her that it was more than all right.

"Exactly what I wanted! Now we can relax. It won't matter so much if I fall under a bus... my understudy can just take over!"

"Don't," begged Caitlyn. "You shouldn't joke about things like that."

I wasn't! Not that I had any intention of falling under a bus. But I definitely wasn't joking.

"Costume-fitting tomorrow," I said. "We'll both have to be there... just in case!"

She pushed at me. "Stop it."

"Fortunately we're about the same size," I said. "So, if I do go and get run over—"

"Stop it, stop it!" She pummelled at me. "It's bad luck to talk like that."

Miss Lucas had made all the costumes herself. She seemed worried that I might not think mine was grand enough.

"Just a plain white leotard and a bit of shredded net for the skirt... what do you think, Maddy? Do you think that's all right?"

I assured her that I thought it was perfect. "After all, I'm supposed to be a bit grubby and worn."

Miss Lucas looked relieved. "That's what I thought! But I did want you to be a little bit glamorous, so how about this? A lovely tiara! There's no reason that should be grubby. And I did wonder, perhaps," she said, "whether we should give you a fairy wand... or maybe not," she added, quickly.

I did hope my face hadn't given me away. "It's just that it wouldn't go with the choreography," I said. "It might sort of... get in the way."

"Of course!" Miss Lucas held up a hand. "Say no more!"

I wondered afterwards if I'd been a bit unkind. She would obviously have liked me to have a wand. A fairy probably *would* have a wand.

"I should have thought about it earlier," I said to Caitlyn. "It would've been easy enough."

"Is it too late?" she wondered. "I mean... would it make much difference?"

I said that it wouldn't if we had more time to practise with it. We only had till the end of the week and I really didn't want to introduce any sort of complication. It wouldn't have bothered *me,* particularly, but it was still something else to cope with, even if it was just a little bit of wand. On the whole it seemed safer not to try.

*　*　*

On Thursday, after school, we had the full dress rehearsal, ready for the performance on Saturday. Livi and Jordan wanted to know if they could come and watch. They seemed to think I was the star of the show and could smuggle them in.

I said, "I'm not the star, I'm just an interlude."

"So who's the star?" said Livi. "Not that great lumping thing from Year Nine?"

She meant the girl who was playing one of the spoilt sisters. I struggled for a moment. The spoilt sisters probably had the biggest parts. But then there was the little boy who rescued the fairy from the gutter. Maybe *he* was the star? In the end I told them that nobody was.

"There aren't any stars; we're all equal."

"But you're the one who'll get all the attention and have her photo in the papers," said Liv.

"Only cos of Mum and Dad," I said. "Not cos of me."

"You're still the most important," said Jordan. "Miss

Lucas thinks you are! I bet you could get us in if you really wanted."

"But all it is is a dress rehearsal," I said. "It'll go on for ages and be really boring. There's loads of technical stuff, like lighting and props, when you just sit around yawning. And then there's people forgetting their lines or saying them all wrong or crashing into the furniture, and everything having to be done over and over until you feel like screaming."

"That's what we want to see," said Liv. "People crashing into the furniture! That's the really interesting part."

"Yes," I retorted, "and it would be most off-putting! You don't want an audience until you feel ready for it. That's why it's called a *rehearsal*. So you can try things out before members of the public are allowed in."

"In the West End," said Jordan, "they have previews. Like before the show properly opens? Members of the public can go to those."

I tried not to feel irritated cos, after all, what did she and Livi know? They weren't in show business. Patiently I explained that a dress rehearsal was not a preview.

"It's just for the actors and people who are helping."

"So how come she gets in?" said Liv.

I said, "Who?"

"*Her.*" Liv pointed. I turned, and saw Caitlyn slipping through the double doors into the hall.

"She's my understudy," I said.

Jordan gave a little snort. "How can she be your understudy when she doesn't even do ballet? Poppy Johnson is ever so upset!"

Poppy was the pudding face I'd been forced to use last year. She really, honestly cannot dance.

"She may not come up to *your* high standards," said Liv, "but you could at least have let her do a little something."

"Could have made *her* your understudy."

"Dunno what she wants an understudy for, anyway," said Liv. "Looks perfectly healthy to me."

 177 ☆

"Specially as it's only one performance. What's going to happen in one performance?"

"Nothing," said Liv. "She could just as well have used Poppy."

The two of them went off together, noses in the air. I called after them, down the corridor: "And what happens if I fall under a bus?"

"Good heavens, Maddy!" Miss Lucas had come up behind me. "What brought that on?"

"I was just saying... it's why people have understudies. In case they *do* fall under a bus."

"Please!" Miss Lucas shuddered. "I'd rather not think about it."

"It's all right," I assured her. "Caitlyn knows the part just as well as I do."

"Yes, and next time," said Miss Lucas, "we must definitely include her. I didn't realise she was a dancer. But, for now, let's just get this dress rehearsal under way!"

* * *

Apart from the girl playing the older of the spoilt sisters forgetting her lines and the other one corpsing, or having a fit of the giggles, the dress rehearsal went surprisingly well. Some people say that a good dress rehearsal means a bad performance, but if you ask me that's just superstition. People only say it so that when they have a *bad* dress rehearsal they can say, "Oh, that means a *good* performance!"

At any rate, Miss Lucas wasn't worried. She was all full of beams and congratulations. She said everyone had worked really hard and, "I just know it's going to be a wonderful, wonderful show!"

I asked Caitlyn afterwards what she had thought of it, since she'd just been sitting there, watching. She said, "You know ages ago, when you first told me about it, you said it was yucky? Well, it's not! It's really, really touching and people are going to weep buckets – specially when they see the poor fairy trying to dance like she did when she was young, and she can't manage it, and honestly it's just so sad! And then at the end when the little boy rescues her—"

"I *wish* I could have played that part," I said.

Caitlyn looked at me, wide-eyed. "But then you wouldn't have been able to dance!"

"You could have done it instead," I told her. "You could've danced and I could've played the little boy. I'd make a really good little boy!"

"You mean —" she said it like she couldn't quite believe what she was hearing — "you mean you'd rather be an actor than a dancer?"

"Well... n-no. I'd like to be both! I'd like to act *and* dance."

"But that's exactly what you're doing," said Caitlyn. "You *are* acting and dancing. You're acting being sad and tired."

"Mm..." I thought about it. I knew that she was right. I had to act *really hard* at being sad and tired. Being a little boy would just have been fun. Being one of the spoilt sisters would have been even more fun! Maybe next year, I thought, Caitlyn *could* do any dancing that was needed and just for once I could be one of the actors. Cos by then, fingers crossed, Caitlyn would be having proper ballet lessons...

Mum had promised to drive me into school on Saturday afternoon, ready for the evening performance. Miss Lucas wanted us all to be there promptly at half past five, but at quarter past Mum was still not home and I was starting to get agitated. It's very unprofessional to be late! Mum herself had taught me that. Fortunately she arrived just a few minutes later, full of apologies.

"One of the mothers wanted to stay and talk to me. I just couldn't get rid of the woman! Don't worry, we'll be there in good time. It's a pity your dad's not here... He says he's heard from Sean that we've got another choreographer in the family!"

I was sorry about Dad, cos I was secretly rather proud of my dance interlude, but Mum was the really important one. She was the one we had to impress.

"You won't be late, will you?" I said, as she dropped me off at the school gates.

"Of course I won't be late! I'm just popping home to put my feet up for five minutes and have a drink, then I'll be coming straight back. I've promised your dad I'll give him a full r—" Mum broke off as her car phone buzzed. "Well," she said, "that's timely! Hallo, Jen, just give me a sec. Off you go, Mads! Break a leg. I'll see you later."

I walked on up the drive, into school. There were posters all over the place announcing *Coombe House Christmas Entertainment*, with little drawings of paper chains and Chinese lanterns and an old-fashioned Christmas tree all hung about with sparkly stuff, with a fairy perched on the top. There were also a few cars in the car park, though I think they were staff rather than parents. We still had over an hour before the show began.

Backstage was buzzing with activity. Miss Lucas scurried past me, down the corridor.

"Ah, Maddy, there you are!" she cried. There was a note of relief in her voice, like she really had expected me to fall under a bus. Just for a moment I felt a little quiver of doubt. Was I doing the right thing? I really didn't want to upset her!

On the other hand there are times when you just have to go for it. When you simply can't help upsetting someone. It all depends what you're upsetting them *for*. I was the one who'd lectured Caitlyn about making the most of every opportunity; I couldn't back out now! I'd never forgive myself.

The dressing room – one of the classrooms next to the hall – was full of people frantically pulling on costumes, prinking and preening in front of mirrors, fussing about their hair or their make-up. Someone was trying to squeeze a big red spot on her chin, someone else had trodden on the hem of her dress and torn it and was wailing pathetically for Miss Lucas, while the younger of the spoilt sisters was hyperventilating in the corner.

"What's her problem?" I said.

"She can't remember any of her lines!"

"Oh," I said, "is that all?"

Everyone stopped what they were doing and turned, reproachfully, in my direction. They all seemed to think I was being heartless. Perhaps I was, but it was *so* unprofessional! Someone pointed out that it was all very well for me: "You don't have to bother with lines."

I thought no, and I didn't have anyone to prompt me, either. Who was going to help *me* if I forgot my steps? Not that I would. But a beginner might, even if she did keep her brains in her feet. Another little quiver of doubt ran through me. I shook it off, impatiently. I couldn't lecture Caitlyn about wasting opportunities and then do the same thing myself. There are times when you just have to take a chance.

Quickly I changed into leotard and tights, twisted my hair back into a bun and sat down to do my make-up. Full ballet make-up is quite dramatic, but you don't really need much in a small school hall. Sheena Walker, who was playing the older sister, watched me in wonderment.

"Is that all you're doing?" *She* was all made up like

something out of a pantomime. "You haven't even touched your eyes, hardly! Would you like me to do them for you?"

"No, thank you." I backed away quickly, before she could get at me.

She shrugged. "Well, it's up to you."

Really, people in Year Nine seem to think they know everything. It's quite annoying. Fortunately Miss Lucas came in at that moment.

"Oh, my goodness!" she cried. "What on earth have you done to yourself, Sheena? Let's get all that make-up scrubbed off and start again."

I took the opportunity, while Miss Lucas was busy, to slip out of the dressing room and go for a bit of a wander. On the way back I went up the steps at the far side of the stage and peered out through a gap in the curtains, trying to see if I could spot Mum. She didn't seem to have arrived yet, but the curtain wasn't due to go up for another twenty minutes. I could see Caitlyn and her mum, though, halfway up the hall. I'd made Caitlyn *promise* to get there in good time.

"You don't want to be stuck right at the back!"

Slowly I returned to the dressing room. Caitlyn was there; Mum would be there soon. It was time to put my plan into action! Limping, I made my way along the corridor. Gritting my teeth with every step. Getting into the part. I'd wanted an acting role, hadn't I? So now I'd got one. This was it! Up to me to prove what I could do.

With a dramatic groan I flung open the door and collapsed on to the nearest chair, clutching my right ankle.

"Maddy!" Miss Lucas came flying over. "What's wrong?"

I gave another groan. "I've done something to my ankle."

"Show me! Let me see. Where does it hurt?"

"Here." I pressed with my fingers. "Ouch! I think I might have pulled a tendon."

"What happened?" said Miss Lucas.

"I was coming down the steps at the side of the stage and I slipped and... ow! It's really painful."

The dressing room had suddenly gone very quiet. People had stopped squeezing spots and wailing about torn hems. This was a crisis!

"I'm sorry," I whispered. "I don't think I'm going to be able to go on."

There were sharp intakes of breath all over the dressing room. I could see the disappointment in Miss Lucas's face, though very quickly she tried to hide it.

Someone said, "Perhaps if you just sat there for a bit?"

Miss Lucas shook her head. "Not if it's a tendon. Do you really think that's what it is, Maddy?"

"I'm not sure. It feels as if it might be. But it's all right!" I said. "Caitlyn's here. She can take my place."

Someone said, "*Caitlyn?*"

"She's my understudy," I said.

And then, quite suddenly, I had another moment of

doubt. Did I really want to do this? My very first piece of choreography and I was going to let someone else dance it?

"On the other hand —" I wobbled to my feet and took a cautious step — "p'raps it's not quite as bad as I thought. Maybe I *could* go on?"

"No! I'm sorry," said Muss Lucas, "but I can't afford to let you take the risk. Not if it's a tendon. What would your mother say?"

"She'd probably say just dance through it... look!" I put my foot on the ground. "Already it's not hurting as much."

"Maddy, please," said Miss Lucas. "Don't argue with me. You were the one who decided — very professionally! — that you should have an understudy. And just as well, as it's turned out! I take it she's here?"

I said, "Yes, but—"

"No buts! Sarah—" Miss Lucas beckoned to the Year Eleven playing the spoilt sisters' mum. "Go into the hall and see if you can find Caitlyn Hughes. Tell her she's needed urgently backstage. And you, Maddy, sit still and stop fretting. There's nothing you can do. These things happen."

I sank back, defeated. It seemed it was too late to change my mind. I was too good an actor!

Sarah arrived back in the dressing room with an ashen-faced Caitlyn. I could see, just from a quick glance, that she was terrified. Miss Lucas said, "Ah, Caitlyn, thank goodness! We're all relying on you. Maddy's hurt her ankle, but she assures me you're more than capable of taking over."

Caitlyn sent me this agonised look. She said, "*M-me?*"

"You can do it!" I said. "You know you can!"

"But... what happened?"

I gritted my teeth, as if in pain. "Fell down the steps at the side of the stage. Just stupid, *stupid*!"

"Do you think you've sprained it?"

"Dunno what I've done." I winced. "It's really painful!" And then bravely I added, "I suppose I *could* try to dance through it..."

"No!" Miss Lucas stepped in, very firmly, just as I'd known she would. "I can't have you putting your whole future at risk. Your mother would never forgive me. If Caitlyn doesn't feel she can do it, we'll just have to cut the dance scene altogether."

I could see Caitlyn's mouth begin to pucker. She looked at me, helplessly.

"Are you really sure?"

No! I wasn't! I was already beginning to have second thoughts. Caitlyn was obviously petrified. Suppose I was making a huge mistake?

"Maybe you could just walk it through," said Sheena. "You, I mean." She nodded at Caitlyn. "I guess it would be better than nothing."

I could see Miss Lucas seriously considering the idea. Caitlyn, too. I suddenly felt a bit desperate. What was I doing? I must have been mad! I felt like springing to my feet and crying, "It's all right, it's all right, don't worry, I'll go on!"

There was this little selfish voice inside my head

urging me to put a stop to things while I still could. Mum was going to be out there and I wanted so much for her to see what I could do! I wanted her to report to Dad how brilliant I was. *It looks like your daughter is going to follow in your footsteps... a budding choreographer!* But, instead, I found myself quite sternly telling Caitlyn how she could dance the part every bit as well as I could.

"You know you can! I wouldn't ask you if I didn't think you could do it. You did bring your shoes," I said, "didn't you?"

She nodded, dumbly. I'd told her that she had to, "just in case".

"You're my *understudy*," I said. "This is why people *have* understudies!"

Miss Lucas said, "Maddy—"

"She can do it!" I said.

I knew I was being a bit of a bully. Maybe there is more of Mum in me than I realise! But sometimes, as Mum is forever telling me, you have to be cruel to be kind. At any rate, that's her excuse for reducing people to tears.

I thought for a moment that I was going to reduce Caitlyn to tears. But then she drew a deep breath, long and quivering.

"I'd better get changed," she said.

By the time she was in costume and I was back in my ordinary clothes, she was shaking so much her teeth were chattering and Miss Lucas was looking really worried. I was feeling pretty worried myself. I thought, *Please, Caitlyn, PLEASE! Don't let me down now!*

"I'm going to go and sit out front with your mum," I said.

"And I'm going to go and find *your* mum," said Miss Lucas, "and tell her what's happening. Or maybe you ought to be the one?"

"Oh, no, please! You do it," I begged. The last thing I wanted was to have to talk to Mum. She'd be bound to ask awkward questions and, in spite of being such a good actor, I wasn't sure she'd be as easy to convince as Miss Lucas.

"Just remember," I whispered to Caitlyn, "brains in your feet!"

The last thing I saw as I hobbled out of the dressing room was her little woebegone smile. I did so hope I'd done the right thing!

Chapter Ten

Miss Lucas insisted on accompanying me as I hobbled into the hall in search of Caitlyn's mum. She had my arm in a grip of iron.

"It's all right, I've got you! Whatever you do, don't put too much weight on that foot."

"I'm trying not to," I said; and I limped elaborately to prove it. It did make me feel a bit self-conscious, cos I mean, people were all looking at me, but then I told myself that I had pulled a tendon and that pulled tendons could be really painful. I remembered when Sean had done it. He had insisted on still going on and dancing through the pain and had ended up in agony. *Ow! Ouch!* It *was* agony. Every time my foot just touched the ground, I could almost feel streaks of fire shooting up my leg.

If you use your imagination, you can make yourself believe all sorts of things. It is what's called *acting*. Getting into the part. By the time we found Caitlyn's mum, I was so into the part that I collapsed with a genuine groan on to Caitlyn's empty chair.

"Now just stay put," said Miss Lucas. "I don't want you up and about on that foot! I'm going to go and find your mum and tell her what's happening."

Caitlyn's mum, looking almost as anxious as Caitlyn herself, said, "Maddy, what have you done?"

"Just pulled a tendon," I said. "It's no big deal but it's not something you should really dance through cos it'll only make things worse. Just as well I have an understudy!"

Caitlyn's mum was obviously confused. She said, "I don't understand! How can Caitlyn be your understudy? She doesn't dance!"

I assured her mum that she did. "I've been teaching her. She's really talented!"

"Really?" Mrs Hughes crinkled her forehead. "Why hasn't she ever said anything?"

I couldn't say, "Because she didn't want to worry you." I'd promised Caitlyn. But I had to say something! Her mum was plainly puzzled.

"I think she wanted to surprise you," I said.

It didn't make much sense but at that moment the lights started to dim and the hall fell silent. I craned forward to see if Mum was there. I knew where she'd be sitting – in the front row, next to Mrs Henson, our headmistress. Guest of honour, that was Mum! And yes, there she was, her red hair glinting. I settled back into my seat with a sigh of relief. The first two parts of my plan had worked! Smooth as could be. The third was up to Caitlyn.

I do believe I was more jittery waiting for her to make her entrance than I have ever been for myself. I am just not a jittery type. But that evening, sitting out front, with nothing to do but watch, I found my heart was thumping. I could sense that Caitlyn's mum, next to me, was even more nervous than I was. I whispered to her that Caitlyn didn't make an appearance until about halfway through, hoping that might help her relax, but I don't think it did. It didn't me, either!

As the first strains of Albinoni's beautiful *adagio* finally stole into the auditorium, and the spotlight centred on the lone figure of the Christmas tree fairy, so sad and so fragile, I found myself holding my breath, my hands bunching themselves into two tight fists. I heard Caitlyn's mum, at my side, draw in a sharp breath.

"It's all right," I whispered. "She'll be all right."

And she was! I think that deep down I'd always known that she would be. For a few terrible moments I was scared that it might all fall to pieces. Her first few steps were so unsteady that I held my breath, awaiting disaster. But then, just as I'd predicted, her feet took over, and from that point on she never looked back. The part might almost have been written specially for her! Who knew? Perhaps it had been. Perhaps all along it was Caitlyn I'd had in mind.

Needless to say, her Christmas tree fairy was very different from mine. Mine would have been so intent on trying to recapture the days of her youth, so determined to push herself to the very limit, that her final collapse would have been a moment of high drama. Caitlyn's whole performance was gentler; more yearning. Even I, at the end, felt moved.

I'd always thought Miss Lucas's story was a bit wimpy and cloying. Caitlyn, on the other hand, had always assured me it would have people in tears. She had been right; I was willing to admit it. And Sean had been right, too: it was definitely Caitlyn's part. But I was still the choreographer! They were my steps; nothing could take that away from me. I had every right to feel proud! And maybe, when Dad was back, I'd be able to show him.

As the curtain came down at the end of the show, I had the feeling that it was Caitlyn most people were applauding. Everyone had been good, but she was the star.

Her mum was obviously still trying to make sense of

things. "Did you really teach her to do all that?" she whispered.

"Well, I was the one who made up the steps –" I couldn't resist telling her – "but mostly Caitlyn taught herself. She's been doing it for ages! What she really needs, before it's too late, are proper lessons."

I felt I could say that now Mum knew what Caitlyn was capable of. Mum is not unreasonable; she just has a horror of pushy ballet mothers thrusting their pudding-faced daughters at her. But now she'd seen Caitlyn for herself, I was sure I could rely on her to come up with a solution. Mum would never let real talent go to waste! Not if she could help it.

I said to Mrs Hughes that I had to go and talk to Caitlyn and find my mum and went racing off down the hall, quite forgetting about my pulled tendon.

"Mum—"

I stopped. Where was she? Where was Mum? I could see Mrs Henson – I could see the person sitting next to her. I'd thought it was Mum, but it wasn't!

"Maddy!" Miss Lucas had appeared, all fussed and bothered cos I wasn't sitting down. "What are you doing? You shouldn't be putting any weight on that foot!"

"I'm looking for Mum," I said.

"Ah, yes! I'm afraid your mum wasn't able to get here after all, but—"

Mum hadn't got here? I couldn't believe it! After all the trouble I'd gone to – the sacrifice I'd made! It should have been *me* they were clapping. *Me* who was the star! *Me* dancing *my* steps that *I* had choreographed. I'd given it all up for nothing!

I became reluctantly aware that Miss Lucas was still talking.

"...managed to get here instead, so we feel very honoured! He's backstage now, congratulating Caitlyn. She did so well! Don't you think? And she says it's all due to you! But Maddy, I'm really worried about your foot; we thought it best to call a cab to t—"

"Hey, Beanie!"

I spun around. "*Sean! Where's Mum?"

★ 200 ☆

"Mum sends her apologies. It seems babies don't always come at the most convenient of times. She had a call from Jen at the last minute and had to go whizzing off to the hospital."

For a *baby*? She'd missed Caitlyn's performance just for a *baby*?

"Honestly," said Sean, "she felt really bad about it."

I scowled. "Oh, now, come on!" He gave me a hopeful grin. "Don't be too hard on her. What d'you expect? It is her first grandchild."

I refused to be comforted. All my sacrifice for nothing! Crossly I said, "So what are you doing here? Why aren't you dancing?"

"Change of schedule. Stop looking so grumpy! I was hoping I'd be an acceptable substitute. You were right about your little friend, by the way! That was a cracker of a performance. Told you, didn't I, that was her sort of part?"

I said, "Yes, and you also told me the only way I could get Mum to take any notice was by letting her think it was *her* idea rather than mine."

"Oh. Right." He nodded, slowly. "Now I get it. Pulled tendon, eh? I thought it seemed a bit unlikely. I take it you've quite recovered?"

"It was all part of my plan," I said, crossly. "I had it all worked out! I might just as well not have bothered what with people having babies all over the place!"

"Absolutely," said Sean. "Very inconsiderate."

I looked at him, uncertainly. Was he being serious?

"Could at least have waited," he said, "till the performance was over."

Just joking. Presumably. For my part I'd have thought *Mum* could have waited. She didn't even like babies! She'd done nothing but grumble ever since Jen got pregnant.

"I feel very hurt," said Sean. "I thought you'd be pleased to see me!"

"I am, but I needed Mum to be here! I went and told Caitlyn's mum that Caitlyn really needs to have lessons and I faithfully *promised* Caitlyn I wouldn't say anything and now her mum's going to be upset and Caitlyn's going to be upset and think I've broken my promise, which I know I have, but only cos I thought Mum was going to be here and—"

"Hey, hey!" Sean put his arms around me. The hall was still full of people and Mrs Henson would probably have said we were making a spectacle of ourselves, though maybe, as it was Sean, she would have forgiven us. People seem to forgive Sean almost anything.

"All is not lost," he said. "*I* was here – *I*'ve seen what she's capable of."

I wailed, "Yes, but you're not Mum!"

"True, but aren't you always accusing me of being her favourite?"

"You are!" He always had been. It was totally gross.

"In that case... why not let me deal with it?"

I looked at him, hopefully. "You mean you'll speak to her?"

"I'll do more than just speak to her. I'll make sure that she listens! Trust me." He tilted my face towards him. "Do you trust me?"

I nodded. If anyone could get through to Mum, it was Sean.

"But please," I begged, "could you do it as soon as we get back? Cos I really don't want Caitlyn's mum telling her what I said and Caitlyn thinking I've betrayed her and—"

"Hush, hush, hush!" He put a finger to my lips. "If Mum is back from the hospital, I'll have a word immediately."

"And you'll ask her if she'll make a scholarship, or something, so Caitlyn's mum doesn't have to be worried?"

"Oh, I shall instruct her," said Sean. "*This is no pudding face*, I shall say. *This is a star in the making! It's your duty – nay, your BOUNDEN duty—*"

"Sean!" I pummelled at him. "Don't make fun!"

"I'm not making fun, you idiot, I'm serious. I have to tell you I'm really impressed with what you've achieved, the pair of you. OK? OK! So, give us a smile... that's better! Now let's go and see if this cab's turned up and whether Caitlyn and her mum would like to be dropped off. And, while we're about it, a bit of heroic limping wouldn't be out of place. You're supposed to have pulled a tendon, right?"

I limped my way obediently to the dressing room to pick up Caitlyn and her mum, then hopped and hobbled, with Sean's help, to find the cab that Miss Lucas had called for us. Caitlyn's mum seemed a bit overwhelmed and kept saying, "You really don't have to," but Sean insisted.

"We can't let the star of the show walk home under her own steam!"

Caitlyn blushed to the roots of her hair. "It should've been Maddy," she said. "I feel so awful about it!"

"Wasn't your fault," I told her. "Just me being clumsy."

"Absolutely," said Sean. "No need to beat yourself up. An opportunity came your way and you took it. That's what it's all about."

"I'd have been well upset," I said, "if you hadn't!"

Mum was waiting for us when we arrived home.

"Maddy, I'm so sorry!" she cried. "You can blame your sister. She was almost a week early!"

Sean pulled a face. "Like I said, grossly inconsiderate. I take it it's all over?"

"Yes, she's got a little boy! James Ivor. I promised we'd all look in tomorrow and say hallo. Is that all right?"

Sean shrugged. "I guess."

"What do you mean, you guess? Don't you *want* to see your nephew? Imagine, you're an uncle and aunt! How cool is that?"

"Yeah, cool," said Sean.

I plucked urgently at his sleeve. Maybe tomorrow I would think it cool to be an aunt at only eleven years old, but right at this moment there were more important matters to be sorted.

"So, how did it go?" twinkled Mum. She was all happy and beaming. Whoever would have thought it? "Did it go well? I'm so sorry I missed it!"

"Actually," said Sean, "you didn't miss the Bean cos she didn't go on."

"What? Why?" Mum looked at me, sharply. "What happened?"

"I kind of—" I sent a pleading glance in Sean's direction. Did I tell Mum the truth or was I still pretending?

"To be honest," said Sean, "it's a long story."

"So tell me!"

"OK. Well, she has this friend, Caitlyn?"

"Yes, yes, I remember! She came to tea."

"Right. And you were supposed to take one look at her and say, *That girl is a dancer.*"

"Oh! That one," said Mum.

"Precisely," said Sean. "That one. But in your inimitable fashion—"

"Excuse me?"

"—you singularly failed to notice. So, most heroically, this one here—" he pulled me towards him, "—decided the time had come for action. It's OK, kiddo, you can stop with the limping."

"Limping?" said Mum. "What limping? What has she done?"

"Put on a most convincing performance," said Sean. "She's a very good actor, aren't you? She certainly hoodwinked poor old Miss Thingummy. Frightened the life out of her. *Oh, dear, I think I may have pulled a tendon.*"

Mum's eyes narrowed to pinpoints.

"You pretended to have injured yourself?"

"Mum," I pleaded, "I had to do something! It was the only way I could think of to get your attention. You're the one that's always saying it's criminal to waste talent!"

Mum switched her gaze to Sean. "*Does* she have talent?"

"She absolutely does," said Sean. "And it *would* be a crime to let it go to waste."

"So what am I expected to do? I take it you've hatched some kind of plan between you?"

"We thought the best solution would probably be a scholarship," said Sean.

"Oh, you did, did you?"

"I know you don't usually give them, but..."

"There's always a first time," I pleaded.

 208 ☆

"Maddy, I am trying to run a business," said Mum.

Sean shrugged. "Well, if you'd sooner have a class full of rich pudding faces..."

There was a pause. Sean closed his hand over mine and squeezed it. Mum frowned.

"You're really telling me she's that good?"

"I'm really telling you," said Sean.

I could see that Mum was beginning to weaken. Eagerly I rushed back in.

"Mum, I've been teaching her! She was having all this trouble with pirouettes and I showed her how to do them, and now I'm giving her lessons every day!"

"Omigod," Mum groaned. "Heaven only knows what faults you'll have let her develop!"

I was about to protest indignantly that I knew better than to let Caitlyn develop bad habits, but Sean got in ahead of me.

"I honestly didn't see any," he said. "Her technique might not be the most secure but for natural ability you couldn't fault her."

"No? Well... perhaps if we get to her in time all may not be lost. You'd better bring her along with you on Tuesday," said Mum. "I'll take a look and see what I think. Oh, and her mum had better come, too, just in case. If she's as exceptional as you seem to think, we'll need to have a talk."

At last! I flew at Sean and hugged him.

"Thank you, thank you, thank you!"

"Don't thank him too soon," warned Mum. "I'm still reserving judgement."

But now I had no doubts. If Caitlyn could get up on stage and dance in front of the whole school, not to mention all the parents and grandparents, she could dance in front of Mum; and, once Mum had seen her, I knew she wouldn't be able to resist. Sean's word alone would probably have been good enough. All the same, I felt it wouldn't hurt to give Caitlyn a few words of encouragement.

* * *

"Forget who it is," I urged Caitlyn, as we waited together the following Tuesday. "Just dance! There's nothing to be scared of; you did all right when it was Sean, and he's every bit as critical as Mum."

"But I didn't know he was there!" wailed Caitlyn. "I'd have died if I'd known!"

I said, "I should hope you wouldn't cos that would've been letting yourself down. *And* it would've been letting me down. Now it'll be letting Sean down, as well! It's only cos of him that Mum's agreed to see you. She never takes any notice of *me*. He was the one that persuaded her. *He* said you gave a cracker of a performance and have natural ability. So there!"

And then I did something I never do: I went all silly and soft and hugged her.

"I know it *is* a bit scary, but just remember... brains in your feet!"

Mum wouldn't let either me or Caitlyn's mum into the studio while she was auditioning Caitlyn, but when they came out Caitlyn was beaming broadly and Mum told Mrs Hughes that she'd like to have a word with her, so I knew at once that things had worked out.

"I have to say," said Mum, as we drove home afterwards, "your brother certainly knows what he's talking about. That girl is one of the most naturally gifted I've seen in a long time."

I said, "Oh! Do you really think so?" Like it wasn't something I'd been trying to tell her for ages.

"I simply can't imagine," said Mum, "how she's got this far without ever having any lessons."

"Except from me," I said.

"Except from you," agreed Mum. "*How* long have you been teaching her?"

"Just a couple of months," I said.

"Well! You've certainly done an excellent job."

I glowed. "What did you say to her mum?"

"I told her straight out it was imperative she started lessons right away. Leave it any longer and it would be too late."

"And did she agree?"

"Oh, I didn't give her any choice," said Mum. "I wasn't taking no for an answer! Not with a talent like that. I've invented a special scholarship for her. Two classes a week, starting next Tuesday. She'll soon catch up."

One thing about Mum: once you've got her attention, she doesn't waste any time.

Caitlyn, when we met at school next day, was in a state of bubbling excitement.

"I can't believe it! I just can't believe it!"

She kept saying it, over and over, in tones of wonderment. We'd spent half the previous evening texting each other. She'd even *texted* me that she didn't believe it! And here we were, the following morning, and it seemed like it still hadn't properly sunk in.

"It's been one of my daydreams," she said, "going to ballet school! Especially your *mum's* ballet school. I just never thought it would happen! And it's all thanks to you! If you hadn't discovered me that day in the gym – if you hadn't made me be your understudy – if you—" She broke off, her face puckering. "Maddy, I never asked you how your ankle was!"

"Don't worry about my ankle," I said. "It wasn't anything. I've forgotten about it. I'm just so happy to think that one of your daydreams has finally come true!" And then, cos I couldn't help being curious, I said, "Do you have lots of others?"

"Lots of daydreams?" She blushed. "Only one."

"Is it to do with ballet?"

She blushed a bit more. "Maybe."

"A particular part that you want to dance?"

"Mm... maybe."

"A particular *person* you want to dance it with?"

She wriggled uncomfortably.

"It is," I said, "isn't it? It's someone you want to dance with!"

"Not telling you."

"Why not?"

"Cos I'm not."

"That's not fair!"

"I know, but you'll laugh."

"I won't!"

"You will cos it's silly. And anyway it can't ever happen."

"You don't know that!"

"I do," said Caitlyn.

"Just tell me who it is," I begged. "*I'll* tell you if I think it's silly."

She shook her head. It didn't matter how much I pleaded with her, she wouldn't budge. But I reckoned I could guess! There was only one person whose name could make her blush like that. I was almost tempted to say it, just to tease her; but then I thought maybe that would be unkind. We should all be allowed to have our secret dreams.

I said, "Well, OK, if you don't want me to know, you don't want me to know. But just promise me one thing... if it ever *does* come true, you'll tell me!"

She nodded, solemnly. "I will."

"You promise? On your honour?"

"On my honour," said Caitlyn. "You'll be the first to know!"

More fantastic reads from Jean Ure…

STRAWBERRY CRUSH

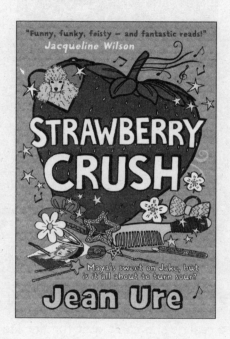

When Mattie's head-in-the-clouds cousin Maya
develops a crush of epic proportions, it's up
to Mattie to make her see sense – Maya will try
anything to be noticed by Jake, even if it makes
her look ridiculous! Will Mattie get through
to Maya before her heart is broken forever?

SECRETS AND DREAMS

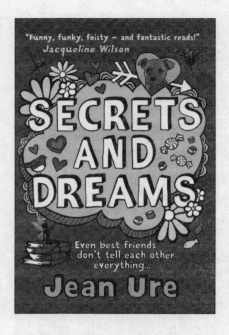

When Zoe's dream of going to boarding school becomes a reality, she can't wait for her life there to begin – but when one of Zoe's new friends reveals a secret too big to share with the others in the group, Zoe finds herself caught in the middle. Staying loyal while 'fitting in' has never seemed harder…

JELLY BABY

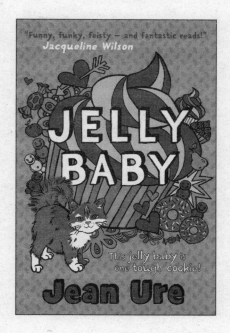

Bitsy, or 'Jelly Baby' as she's sometimes called,
has been doing just fine living with Dad and big sister
Em since Mum died. Until one day Dad brings
home a girlfriend and everything changes.
Now it's down to the Jelly Baby of the family
to keep it from falling apart...

Salvatore d'Amato is determined to get a kiss by
his thirteenth birthday. And not just any kiss.
A kiss from his heart's desire – the 'lovely, loveable,
luscious Lucy'! With his wonderful love poetry,
and his secret body-building, how will she be able
to resist? If only that horrible Harmony Hynde
would stop bothering him in the meantime!

JUST PEACHY

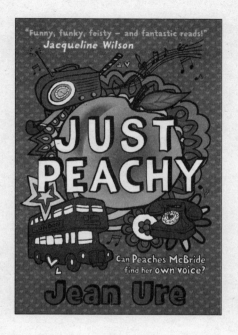

I'm the quiet one in my very loud family.
Not a drama queen, or a genius, but Just Peachy.
When I went to choose my own school, everyone
finally stops to listen! Stepping out on my own
is scary, but if I want to figure out who I am
maybe scary is just what I need...

SECRET MEETING

Mum has always warned me that people you
meet in chatrooms aren't always what they seem.
But when my best friend Annie meets my favourite
author Harriet Chance online and arranges tea,
it's the best birthday present ever! Until Mum's
warning starts to come true...